AN UNACCEPTABLE DEATH

OTHER BOOKS IN THE
MUNCH MANCINI CRIME NOVEL SERIES

Unwilling Accomplice
Unpaid Dues
No Man Standing
Unfinished Business
Unwanted Company
No Offense Intended
No Human Involved

BARBARA SERANELLA

AN UNACCEPTABLE DEATH

THOMAS DUNNE BOOKS ST. MARTIN'S MINOTAUR NEW YORK

THOMAS DUNNE BOOKS.
An imprint of St. Martin's Press.

www.minotaurbooks.com

Library of Congress Cataloging-in-Publication Data

Seranella, Barbara.
An unacceptable death / Barbara Seranella.—1st ed.
p. cm.
ISBN 0-312-34798-7
EAN 978-0-312-34798-7
1. Mancini, Munch (Fictitious character)—Fiction. 2. Women detectives—California—Fiction. 3. Automobile mechanics—Fiction. 4. Police murders—Fiction. 5. California—Fiction. 6. Revenge—Fiction. I. Title.

PS3569.E66U53 2006
813'.54—dc22

2005053727

First Edition: January 2006

10 9 8 7 6 5 4 3 2 1

FOR DR. TSE-LING FONG

ACKNOWLEDGMENTS

THIS IS THE PART WHEN I TRY VERY HARD NOT TO FORGET any of the fine people who helped me with the research and production of this novel.

Here goes:

IA Sheriff's investigator Carl Carter answered many questions. So did my good friend Stephanie Monash. Thank you both for sharing your expertise.

DEA agent Rocky Herron, private investigator Becky Altringer, David Corbett, and sheriff's deputy Gary Bale were helpful with certain facts. My good friend Jerry Hooten gave me a great tutorial on listening devices and body wires, complete with pictures.

My wonderful critique groups: The Orange County Fictionaires; and John, Rachel, Tom, Grahame, and Sheila of our intimate Coachella Valley critique group. I treasure both groups' wisdom, companionship, and humor.

Thanks are also in order to my wonderful agent Sandra Dijkstra and staff; my publicists and friends Debbie Mitsch and Nanette Heiser of Martin and Mitsch; and my wonderful husband, Ron, who sticks with me through sick and sin.

PART ONE
BEFORE AND AFTER

CHAPTER ONE

MUNCH LIKED RICO'S HAIR LONGER. SHE ALSO DUG THE FU Manchu mustache he had grown, but she was glad he'd given up on the scraggly beard. Mexican men should stick to mustaches.

It was Saturday. Asia, Munch's nine-year-old daughter, was at her dance class. Rico had surprised her with his visit, but that's the way they had to play it—snatching moments together when they could.

They strolled down the sidewalk, Rico's arm resting comfortably on her shoulders. He was a foot taller than her own five feet. They fit together just right.

If she had lived in a nicer neighborhood, she would have warned her neighbors that this *vatto*-looking guy was really a cop and in disguise. But between the bikers across the street, the houseful of probably illegal aliens next to them, the crazy Okie next door with the inbred daughter, and the alcoholic divorcée on the other side, it was probably safer for all concerned to say nothing.

Her WWII-vintage bungalow home was in Santa Monica, on a street lined with untrimmed palm trees and a few Spanish-style quasi-adobe houses that had seen better days. This part of Santa Monica was closer to the gang-bangers of Venice than the pricey shops on Montana Avenue or the large stately homes on San Vincente Boulevard. Her little slice of real estate was far enough inland to be affordable on her auto mechanic's salary and whatever income could be eked from her limo business. If someone had told her ten years earlier that she would one day be a homeowner, she would have wondered what they were on.

Jasper walked ahead of Rico and Munch with his leash draped across his shoulders. The cocker spaniel looked back frequently to make sure the humans were keeping up.

"I'm thinking of getting some tats," Rico said.

He'd already pierced his ear and had taken to wearing a small gold sliver of moon stud. She considered his brown skin and thought red would look good.

"How about PROPERTY OF MUNCH on your ass?"

"It's already on my heart."

She laughed. "Good answer."

"I'm getting a lot of practice being quick on my feet."

She shuddered against the chill his words brought. It was hard to think of him out there in the war zone. That world was dangerous enough without being a spy for the other side. She pulled away from him and folded her arms across her chest. "How much longer?" she asked, trying to sound neither impatient nor worried or upset.

"I can't say."

She nodded, knowing she would have to be content with that answer and feeling anything but.

He put his arm back around her shoulders and pulled her close. "How long we got before the kid comes home?"

"That I can answer." She made a hand signal to Jasper indicating it was time to turn around and head home. "The better part of an hour."

"I can give you that," he said, picking up Jasper's leash.

"Uh-oh." Munch spotted a pit bull coming their way. The dog was secured by a short chain to its short master; both were bandy-legged and full of attitude. "Enemy approaching."

Jasper was still in happy-go-lucky mode, tail up, mouth open in a dog smile, black eyes liquid and trusting.

The pit bull had scars across his face and back. As he approached, his muscles rippled beneath his short hair. Munch knew the breed had a bite like a piranha and once they'd sunk their teeth in their prey, it was darn near impossible to make them let go. She'd seen the biker across the street use a four-inch nail punch like a hood prop once when his mastiff got hold of another neighbor's cat.

Jasper finally spotted the approaching danger. He puffed out his chest, straightened his forelegs, and pawed the sidewalk with alternating back legs like a bull getting ready to charge. The hair along his spine sprouted into a Mohawk and he barked his deep boy bark.

Rico pulled the leash in tight and waited for the other dog to approach. The pit bull and his master drew alongside them and then stopped, as both dogs snarled and snapped at each other. The two men shortened their leashes and the dogs responded by rising up until both were on their hind legs, lips curled back to reveal sharp white teeth.

Munch wondered why one of the men didn't just keep walking on his way, ending the encounter that much sooner. It would be logical. As if logic dictated the behavior of males in the wild. She also knew Rico wouldn't back down first.

The owner of the pit bull took a second take on Rico. "*Essé*," he said, giving his dog a curt command to sit. "You're Xavier's homie, right?"

Rico tilted his head in a short upward nod and Munch saw him instantly transform into street persona. She knew not to call him by name in case this other guy knew him by something other than Rico.

Rico handed Munch the leash. "Wait here," he said. "We've got a little business to discuss."

Munch assumed the good-ol'-lady pose, taking a few steps back and waiting patiently for her man's pleasure. The more things changed, the more they stayed the same. She'd been pretending in the old days, too, before she had become a respectable citizen.

Rico and the *vatto* communicated in a street mix of English and Spanish. Barrio Spanish. Rico pulled a ballpoint pen refill from his coat pocket and found a scrap of paper on the ground. When he finished writing, he returned the ink cartridge and note to his pocket. After shaking hands like they were arm wrestling, the two he-men parted company. The *vatto* gave Munch an up-and-down as if he were picturing her pinned beneath him with her clothes torn off. She returned the look boldly as if to say, "Not going to happen."

The guy leered knowingly. Munch wanted to kick him in the balls. She saw the top of the Virgin Mary's head on his upper back as he walked away. Guys in prison favored the tattoo, hoping to put a would-be rapist out of the mood. Probably a tactic that only worked with Catholics.

"Who's the charmer?" Munch asked when the guy was out of earshot.

"He invited us to a barbecue," Rico said.

"Oh, great. I'll make some potato salad."

"You'd be better off developing a case of amnesia." He grabbed her arm when they got close to her house and kept them walking past her yard without glancing at it. "Just to be safe," he said.

Munch was all for erring on the side of caution even as part of her was excited by the action. "Nice touch with the pen, by the way," she said. Street toughs didn't carry Parker ballpoints in their shirt pockets like a citizen might.

He chuckled. "It's the little things that keep you alive."

CHAPTER TWO

ON SUNDAY, MUNCH WOKE EARLY. IT WASN'T YET EIGHT, so she let Asia sleep, pulled on her bathrobe, and went outside to retrieve the *LA Times* from her driveway.

Fog shrouded the neighborhood. A fine jeweled mist clung to her roses and beaded the limo's car cover. The fog wouldn't burn off until ten. On weekdays, that was long after she had gone to work in sunnier Brentwood.

She scanned the headlines as she waited for the coffee water to boil. President Reagan was still talking to Soviet leader Mikhail Gorbachev, hopefully not about his polyps. The country had learned last summer, in vivid detail, all about colons, following the president's colonoscopy and subsequent surgery to remove the benign cysts growing within him.

The investigation continued to find out why the space shuttle *Challenger* exploded last month. What a bummer that had been! Munch heard about the disaster at work, and didn't learn until that evening that many elementary-school kids had been watching the broadcast live. Appalled teachers had their students put their heads on their desks, but by then the damage was done. Asia, who wanted to be an astronaut (or a ballerina or a veterinarian) had been really shaken by the tragedy.

In science news, Halley's Comet would be visible this year. The next time it was due around was in seventy-five years. The Griffith Park Observatory was having a special program for kids who would be alive to see it in the year 2061. Thinking of Asia, Munch tore out the article and pinned it to the corkboard above the counter.

She grinned as she went about her morning routine. Rico had promised to come over midday.

After finishing her breakfast and reading the paper, Munch went out back into the narrow slice of her yard and examined her crop of vegetables. She had built the raised plant bed herself. It had taken twenty bags of assorted mulch, potting soil and a lot of other junk the guy at the nursery said was essential to fill the railroad-tie-bordered rectangle. She then studied the path of the sun, the height the mature plants reached, and planted accordingly. She didn't spend much time on the correct season for planting. Los Angeles' weather was so mild, she didn't think it would matter. The only mistake she made was in not understanding the germination process of corn. She was a city girl, after all.

Since corn was the tallest vegetable, she had planted a single row of stalks along the wooden fence that separated her from the Okies. The corn grew straight and over six feet high, but the ears didn't get anywhere as large as the ones she saw at the market. An article she'd read said to harvest the corn when the silk turned brown. She chose that Sunday, so Asia and Rico could share the moment. The same article had also said that the corn was at maximum sweetness when pulled from the stalk and diminished from there as the sugar turned to starch. She figured the corn had cost her ten dollars an ear, not counting labor. It had better be good.

Rico arrived at eleven and Munch assigned him to the barbecue while Asia and Jasper pestered each other with a tennis ball. They were a regular little family now. The man, the woman, the child, the dog. All together for a nice Sunday family cookout.

"How are the coals?" Munch asked Rico.

"What?" called the voice across the fence. It was the Alpha Okie, or at least the lone male of the strange tribe next door.

Munch looked at Rico and rolled her eyes. "Almost there," Rico called back.

"You say something, Daddy?" a female voice across the fence shrieked, sounding pissed off.

"Where's my ladder?" the man responded. Munch knew his name was Earl, but the females next door all called him Daddy. He called two of the women Mother. The youngest female was in her twenties and had teeth growing in every direction. Munch noticed this because on their infrequent encounters the girl never shut her mouth, letting it hang open as she stared. Munch avoided contact with the disturbing clan as much as possible.

Rico mimicked the dueling banjo music from *Deliverance.*

Munch smiled as she picked three of the more promising ears of corn and shucked them. Once the husk and silk were disposed of, she was left with little more than bare cobs. The individual kernels had failed to plump with their promised sweetness.

"Let's see," Rico said.

Munch held up an ear, it wilted pathetically to one side.

Asia pointed one small brown finger at the motley vegetable. "I'm not eating that." There was a touch of hysteria to her voice.

Just when things couldn't get worse, Munch heard the doorbell ring. She went in the back door, walked through the house, Jasper barking at her heels, and opened the front door.

A familiar figure stood on her stoop. Today she was a shaggy brunette with violet eyes, a shade not found in nature. Rhinestones glittered from her fingernails and enough cleavage showed through her skintight leotard body shirt to raise the dead. A black Camaro Z-28 was parked at the curb.

Ellen.

Or, as she was often referred to by people whose lives she'd touched: *Fucking Ellen*.

"I thought I would surprise you." Ellen stretched out every word in that Deep South drawl she'd perfected over the years of living in California.

"You did," Munch said. "You always do."

"We have got to talk, and I mean right now."

Munch could only imagine what Ellen had managed to get herself mixed up in this time.

Ellen swept down to give Jasper some loving. "Where is that other little rug rat of yours?"

"We're out back, fixing to eat." Munch heard her shift of cadence. A couple of hours with Ellen and she'd have the accent too. "Come on." Few people understood why Munch kept opening her door to Ellen. The two women had known each other since puberty. Munch wouldn't have laid odds that they'd both make thirty, but here they were. Ellen was even sober, too. Well, most of the time. Munch didn't press the topic as long as Ellen didn't come around loaded. Of course, she didn't come around all that often either. Probably just as well. She was one of those people best taken in small doses.

Ellen didn't set out to cause trouble everywhere she went. Really she didn't. Ellen had been through the same wars Munch had fought and survived. Ellen did more than survive, she still maintained a sense of optimism. She'd taken her knocks, they all had. It went with the make-it-up-as-you-go and try-not-to-die street life they'd been born to. Ellen had helped make it fun.

The two women had learned early on to pop right back up, usually with a laugh and a plan, and say, "Next." Even at Ellen's dad's memorial service, when a pigeon shit all over her black dress, she'd just glanced over and said, "Could have been worse." Against all odds, her attitude carried her. Attitude was nine-tenths of the battle, no matter what the skirmish.

Munch had pursued the life of drugs so hard that she had been left, at twenty-two, with no viable options other than to get completely clean and sober. It was that or prison or some other institution. But more likely her fate would have been an unmarked grave, and few left to mourn her. Ellen had always maintained a modicum of control, never going completely over the edge, and still had some mischief left in her.

Ellen was closer than blood. Ellen was family by choice and history. Munch would never shut the door on her.

Munch led her out back. Rico was turned away from them, tending the burgers and hot dogs. His hair was pulled back in a small ponytail. Ellen appraised his backside and gave Munch the thumbs-up.

"Put another shrimp on the barbie, mate," she said in good approximation of an Australian accent.

Rico turned. It took him a few seconds to reach Ellen's face. They recognized each other simultaneously. Their smiles transformed into "Oh, it's you" expressions.

"Ellen Summers," Rico said, sounding every bit the cop.

"Auntie Ellen!" Asia yelled and came running into her arms.

"How is my precious angel?" Ellen asked, smoothing Asia's brown curls and tweaking her nose.

"I've been *very* good lately," Asia said with an eye on Ellen's big purse.

Ellen opened her bag and sifted through the twelve pounds of beauty accessories and assorted paraphernalia she felt was absolutely essential to carry with her everywhere. While she searched, she cast another long look at Rico's clothes, hair, and three-day growth of beard. "You working undercover or something?"

"What's your excuse?" Rico shot back.

"Like I need one."

Before Rico could respond, Ellen produced a gift wrapped in balloon-decorated paper and tied with a pink bow. She handed the package to Asia, who tore into it immediately. It was a book with a real silver-plated heart-shaped locket sealed in cellophane in the cover.

"Oh, thank you," Asia said. "It's beautiful."

"You will have to read me the story later," Ellen said. "I think it is time to eat."

"Stick with the meat," Asia said, speaking out the side of her mouth.

Before Ellen had a chance to crack wise, Munch announced, "We've put in an offer on another house."

"A bigger one," Asia added, "for all of us."

"Well, aren't we just the bourgeoises?" Ellen said.

"What does that mean?" Asia asked, always annoyed when she felt adults were excluding her from the conversation.

"Nothing bad," Munch said. "Just that we're moving up in the world. Owning more stuff and making more money."

"Oh." Asia shredded the plastic holding the locket. "That's good." She admired her new piece of jewelry. "When I was little I used to think that when I grew up I would buy lots of money."

Munch and Rico exchanged smiles.

"What's your plan now?" Ellen asked.

Asia wrinkled her nose and nodded sagely. She had obviously given this some thought. "I think I'll marry a millionaire."

Munch choked back an outraged laugh and chucked her farming efforts in the trash can. "I'll go get the condiments."

"You got any of the ribbed kind that glow in the dark?" Ellen asked, following her to the kitchen.

Munch shook her head. "Behave yourself, will you?" Even as she spoke, she realized she was chastising Ellen for Rico's benefit. She wondered if either of them had picked up on it and why was she always being forced to pick sides between the people she loved.

Munch took another plate down from the cabinet.

Ellen arranged the slices of tomato, onion and cheese on a platter, garnishing the outer ring with leaves of lettuce. The girl did have her talents. Munch could spend an hour over the same platter and not come up with anything half so pleasing to the eye.

Munch opened the refrigerator to retrieve the jars of mayo, mustard and ketchup, discreetly flipping over her and Rico's wedding invitation on the corkboard as she set them on the table. She was still working on Rico's veto of Ellen on the guest list. "What do you want to drink?"

"What are my choices?" Ellen asked.

"Coke, apple juice, milk, or water."

"Milk, then."

Munch took out the carton. "They really glow in the dark?"

"Yes, indeed." Ellen marched an upright banana across the kitchen table and sang out, "Here comes the monster."

Munch laughed.

Ellen peeled the banana and took a bite. "So things are getting pretty serious between you and Rico, huh?"

"We've had the keys to each other's houses for six months."

"You going to get married?"

There it was. Trust Ellen to hit on the topic Munch most hoped to avoid.

"I saw your ring," Ellen said.

Well, duh, Munch thought. She'd forgot she was wearing the tiny solitaire diamond on the delicate gold band that Rico had given her a month ago. Guess Ellen didn't have to bc Sherlock to figure that one out. Munch held out her nicked-up, grease-stained left hand. It wasn't as banged up as her right, but the girly ring still looked odd on her finger.

"I only wear it on weekends. I don't want it getting messed up at work." Even now, the diamond setting sported a strand of thread. She pulled the pocket lint free. The ring was pretty, but totally impractical.

"So, have you set a date?" Ellen asked.

"We're closing in on one. I'll let you know." She hoped she wasn't lying. "So how's your love life?"

"Nobody real special, per se. I've been keeping my options open, if you know what I mean."

"Open options can be fun if you don't have a little kid watching your every move."

“Yeah, I can see how that might crimp a person’s style. Not that it isn’t worth it.”

“You still have your condo?” Munch asked the question casually, but what she was really trying to gauge was how well Ellen was managing her inheritance. Both her parents had died within a month of each other and Ellen had been their sole beneficiary. Munch had worried that the windfall would be the end of Ellen, that she’d go on the Cali Cartel diet until there was nothing left of her.

“I’ve got the condo, my car, and a money market account earning nine-and-a-half percent interest. You don’t have to worry about me. This time it’s you that needs worrying after.”

“How’s that?”

“The Pride is reorganizing, trying to get the Venice chapter active again.”

“Great.” The Pride was shorthand for the Satan’s Pride Motorcycle Club. Outlaw motorcycle clubs had a recurrent theme to what they called themselves: Hell’s Angels, Heathens, Pagans, Satan’s Slaves, Devil’s Disciples. Munch had had some bad experiences with the Satan’s Pride just before getting sober. Seems she had transmitted a social disease to a few of the members. They were gang-raping her at the time, so she didn’t feel too terribly guilty about it. Besides, who were they to point fingers as to where a disease originated?

Long story short, to their way of thinking, she had done them wrong. Kind of like a burglar suing the homeowners because he tripped over their furniture in the dark. Instead of taking her to court, the bikers had planned on selling her to a sadistic murderer.

She had turned the tables on them, which resulted in their president, Crazy Mike, being shot dead by the cops and the rest of the pack departing for points unknown.

“It gets worse,” Ellen said. “I heard a rumor that there was a bounty on your ass.”

“For what?’

“You know how those guys are. You embarrassed them.”

“What was I supposed to do? Let them kill me?”

“A good ol’ lady would have.”

They looked at each other and laughed. Neither of them had ever been in contention for Harley Whore of the Year. They were both too opinionated to make the cut. Good biker babes didn’t have a point of view until their men told them what it was.

“How much?” Munch asked.

“Their patch.”

Munch knew that instant membership, without having to go through the year-long initiation of being a prospect, was quite an inducement. “That seems pretty specific for a rumor.”

“Yeah, well.” Ellen picked up the platter and headed for the backyard. “Maybe you sleeping with a cop ain’t such a bad thing after all.”

“I guess that would depend on the cop.”

CHAPTER THREE

THE FOLLOWING THURSDAY, MUNCH STOPPED ON HER way home from work to do some quick shopping at Royal Market on Washington Boulevard. The mom-and-pop grocery store was across the street from the AA clubhouse and one of the few markets left in Los Angeles that dispensed Blue Chip stamps. Munch and Asia were saving for a kitchen clock they'd found in the catalog. It was shaped like an English country cottage and required twelve books of stamps for redemption. She and Asia painstakingly collected and pasted the stamps between the dotted lines of the booklets. They were only half a book short.

Munch unloaded her purchases onto the rubber conveyer belt. Harleys idled out front and she wondered if they were being ridden by anyone she knew. Damned if the choppers' deep-throated rumbles weren't still music to her ears.

The checkout clerk paused. Munch looked up from her purse, expecting a total to be showing on the register.

The clerk wasn't finished. She dangled a wilted piece of vegetation from her fingertips and looked at it as if she wasn't sure it was something she should be touching.

Munch realized with a jolt that it was one of her anemic ears of corn. She blushed deeply and looked behind her. Rico stood there grinning.

"Just throw it away," Munch told the clerk, mortified and amused at the same time. Rico laughed out loud, then kissed Munch on the cheek. She punched his arm. "What are you doing here?"

Rico waited until Munch had paid for her groceries and collected her change and stamps. He picked up the bags and they headed for the exit. "I did some checking on what Ellen said about the Pride looking for you."

"And?"

"She was right."

"Great. Should I be worried?" Munch did feel a little thrill of dread at his words, but then she refused to give in to that reaction on principle. It was much easier to deal with the bad bikers of her past if she focused on her contempt for them rather than giving them the respect of fear. She was also a tiny bit proud to still be a bone in their craw after all this time.

"I think we can put an end to this right away," Rico said.

Munch gestured to the bikes now visible through the market's glass doors. "You gonna turn me in and collect the reward yourself?"

"Even better than that. I've got a silver bullet for you. A magic password."

She opened the door for herself and he followed. "Does it involve clicking my heels together three times and saying 'There's no place like home'?" She glanced at the bikers, but none of them were familiar.

"The dude trying to revamp the chapter is who we go after. His name is Peter Donner. You might have known him as Petey."

"Tall guy?" Munch asked. "Black hair, blue eyes?" Munch opened her trunk and Rico put away the bags.

"So you knew him?"

"Yeah, he thought he was God's gift to women." Actually, Ellen knew him a *lot* better. She said he was nothing special in the sack. Pretty boys rarely were, figuring they were doing you a favor being with you, and therefore you should do all the work.

Rico lowered his voice, speaking softly so that his next words reached only her. "Five years ago, he gave us information that helped bust some Mongols on a murder beef."

"Isn't that supposed to be, like, confidential? When someone snitches?"

Rico shrugged. "If two people know a secret, it isn't a secret."

Munch nodded. Someone always blabbed. It was human nature.

"So, we, like, blackmail him?"

Rico nodded. "The Mongols' lawyer knew there was an informant. He was also privy to the informant's code name, but not his identity."

"What was his code name?"

"The Desert Fox."

"Oh, please. Someone tell this guy to get over himself."

"I think Petey would very much like to keep that information from reaching certain people."

"So we let him know that if something happens to me, his cover will be blown. What's to stop us from dropping a dime on him now?"

"We want him in charge, so we can control the threat to you."

Munch put her arms around Rico's waist and pulled him to her. He didn't resist. "Did anyone ever tell you that you can be very sneaky?"

He smiled and kissed her. "Maybe once or twice."

"How do we get the word to ol' Petey baby?"

"You leave that part to me."

"You're so good to me." Without her usual sarcastic edge, the words caught mid-throat—it was the unexpected truth of them. How did she ever get so lucky?

"This is what it's all about." Rico cupped her face in his hands, smoothing back the skin under her eyes with his thumbs. "I'm your man, of course I'm going to take care of you. You'd do the same for me."

Again, a concept that was alien to Munch, a lover being a help instead of a complication. "You're not making out so good on this bargain," she said. "I've got more baggage than the average bear."

"Don't worry about it." He kissed the top of her head. "I've done my share of shit, too. Just remember, when it comes down to it, it's you and me and the kids."

"Jasper, too."

"Yeah," Rico said, "he's covered under the kid category."

"Will I see you later?"

"I don't know. I'll call if I get a chance."

They kissed once more and then he was gone.

CHAPTER FOUR

JASPER FELL OFF THE BED AND WOKE MUNCH UP. IT SUR-prised her. She always expected animals to be sure-footed and agile, much the way she expected Native Americans to have keen vision. But the reality was she'd met several nearsighted Indians and shared her bed with a clumsy cocker spaniel.

She got up and pulled on her Texaco uniform. Dawn was just breaking as she retrieved her newspaper. The neighborhood was quiet, giving her the illusion that she had the world to herself.

There wasn't anything earth-shattering on the front page. She checked out her horoscope, read some of her favorite comics, and was just turning to the obituaries when there was a knock at the door, sounding louder than normal. Munch looked at the clock, confirming what she already knew. It was too early for good news.

She glanced out the front window on her way to answer the door. Her caller was Mace St. John. He was dressed for work or court in a dark suit. St. John was a homicide detective with the West Los Angeles division of the LAPD. He was also Asia's godfather. Munch had met him in a Venice biker bar when he came to arrest her for the murder of her pimp father, Flower George. That had been nine years and another life ago. The event that marked the beginning of their friendship also heralded her sobriety from drugs and alcohol. And, like many of her adventures in the bad old days, it began in a biker dive and ended in a police station.

Those times were behind her, yet always a part of her. The Program had taught her not to dwell nor shut the door on the past. Embrace the lessons. Remember.

She reached for the doorknob with her left hand, noticing as she always did the faint white scar along the vein that stretched from her wrist to the crook of her arm. Needle marks. Tracks of a right-handed junkie. She'd forever remember that.

"It doesn't look like I woke you," St. John said. He reached for her elbow and held it. This close, even at a stooped five feet ten inches, he towered over her own five feet. She looked into his face. The bags under his eyes seemed more pronounced. He had nicked himself shaving and completely missed a small triangle of whiskers on his chin.

"What's wrong?" she asked.

"I don't have all the details," he said. "It's Rico, honey."

She wanted him to stop right there, to give her another few seconds of happiness before he delivered his news.

"I'm sorry," St. John said. "I got the call this morning."

Munch fought the urge to shut the door in his face.

He still held her arm. "The details are sketchy."

"Wait," she said, but he didn't hear her. Maybe she hadn't spoken out loud.

"Honey," St. John said, "Rico is dead."

Something went *click* inside her. Maybe it was her light switch turning off. She wondered if her heart had stopped, that would explain the sharp pain. *No.* She tried to say the word out loud, but it wouldn't come. She twisted out of St. John's grip and left him standing at the door.

This couldn't be right. She and Rico were in love. They were going to get married. That was the plan. Happily ever after, just like the movies.

The throw blanket on the couch was askew. That was all wrong, too. She shook it out and refolded it; her hands jerked at the task, but she couldn't slow them down.

Asia would have to be told. Munch would hold her out of school today. She'd have to call Lou, her boss at the Texaco station, and explain—

"Munch?" St. John's voice.

She scooted the couch closer to the wall, the lamp on the end table wobbled. St. John caught it before it fell.

"I have to do things," she said.

"Let me help; what do you need?"

"I don't know. I can't think. Wait. I told you to wait." She wanted to hit his face, scratch his eyes out, make him bleed.

He tried to grab her arm again, but she pulled back. "Waiting won't change the facts," he said.

"God forbid we change any facts." She heard the hysterical lilt to her voice, but didn't seem to have any control over volume or tone. *Focus,* she thought. *Deep breath. God, it hurt to breathe.*

St. John patted the couch. "Here, sit."

"I can't." There were details to see to. The realtor would have to be called. She'd withdraw the offer on the new house, stay where she could afford the payments alone.

Alone. The word had an echo to it. And why was she thinking about money now? What kind of a cold-blooded monster was she?

She didn't need to ask St. John if he was sure. He wouldn't be here otherwise. When, how, why? None of that was important either, but he was probably expecting her to ask.

Why would she need to know any of the details? None of those answers would change the fact that Rico was gone, forever. An image of Rico smiling at her floated before her eyes. It was something she would never see again except in her dreams.

Maybe if she went back to sleep? *You're not making sense,* she scolded herself.

"Oh, God, please." She heard the words as she spoke them. She didn't recognize her voice, it was too high, almost otherworldly. Her neck ached, her throat, her chest, but the tears wouldn't release. Tears would help. She'd read that somewhere.

St. John followed her around the room. She fended him off with outstretched hands. She should never have answered the door.

"Caroline's on her way over."

Munch blinked at him, not understanding for a moment the meaning of his words or what they had to do with anything. Caroline, Mace's wife, was Munch's former probation officer and Asia's godmother.

St. John rubbed the back of his neck. "You want me to call anyone else?"

Munch massaged her forehead in an effort to get her brain to work. A question needed answering. "His daughter, Angelica. She lives with his ex-wife." Angelica was going to be devastated. She loved her daddy. They all loved her daddy.

"Someone's going to the house," St. John said gently. "I know you go to work early and I didn't want you hearing about it on the radio."

They had arrived in the kitchen. She looked down at the table where the "Metro" section of the *Times* was spread open. "It wasn't in the paper," she said stupidly, feeling as if she were underwater and pedaling desperately for the surface.

"Not yet," he said. "And I meant is there anyone you want me to call for you?"

Munch thought of her AA sponsor, Ruby. Ruby would want her to go to a meeting and "share her feelings." She wasn't up to sharing shit. The last thing she wanted now was another dose of reality.

"No. There's no one."

What next? She crossed the thin carpet of her living room toward the nook she used as her office, thinking to grab a pen and paper, start a list.

Her eyes refused to focus. The lined pad before her remained blank. She clutched at her scalp, pulling her shoulder-length light-brown hair as if she might literally draw out the needed answers. She thought of the expression "pulling out her hair" and wondered with detachment if this very sort of action/reaction was the origin of that phrase.

Make a note, idiot.

The teapot whistled. She went back into the kitchen and turned off the flame. She didn't want to be more awake. St. John stood in the doorway.

"You want some coffee?"

"You got any decaf?"

He'd given up caffeinated coffee after his heart attack over a year ago.

"No, sorry. Strictly leaded."

"That's all right," he said. He looked uncomfortable. She didn't know what she was supposed to do now either.

"Help yourself to whatever," she said. "I need to hit the head."

He nodded. His sad eyes waited.

She went into the bathroom. Jasper followed her. She closed the door gently behind them, crossed to the sink, and opened the cold water tap.

Now, the voice in her head urged, *do it now.*

She slumped to the floor, covered her face with both hands, and sobbed. Jasper came to her. He was shivering, upset by her emotion. She hugged him to her and cried into his fur, staying that way until there was a soft knock at the front door, and she knew the world was about to intrude.

Rico was dead and it was all her fault. Her universe was divided into two time zones—before and after this terrible news, and the inescapable fact: If he had never met her, he would probably still be alive.

CHAPTER FIVE

CAROLINE ST. JOHN VOLUNTEERED TO TAKE ASIA TO school. Munch had found it surprisingly easy to act as if nothing had happened. Asia accepted the St. Johns's presence without question, relieving Munch of the necessity of lying—a skill that came back all too easily when she needed it.

She kissed Asia good-bye and then returned to the kitchen, where St. John was working on his second cup of herbal tea.

"You'll be getting some calls today," he said. "The criminal investigation team will want to interview you, and a few guys from IA."

IA. Internal Affairs. The cops who policed the cops.

"IA? What's that about?" Munch asked. She grabbed for the box of Raisin Bran, then realized she wasn't the least bit hungry and put it back on the shelf.

"They investigate all officer-involved shootings." St. John looked uncomfortable. "Just be up-front with them. You have nothing to hide, right?"

"Oh yeah, my past is a matter of public record."

"Are you going to be around today?"

"I thought I'd go over to Rico's dad's house and see what I can do for them." She picked up the TO DO list she had begun, but had difficulty reading it. Her letters were misshapen and most of the words had been left unfinished. She took a deep breath. The pain was still there. Maybe it was a part of her now. "How does this work?"

"What do you mean?"

She blinked back tears. "Does the department arrange the funeral? Should I call the coroner's office? I'd like to make it as easy on the family as I can."

St. John seemed to know what she needed and what she didn't. A word of sympathy right now would completely unwind her.

"I'll let you know the timetable as soon as all that is decided," he said. "We usually do a showy funeral for the troops and PR. The hypocrisy is painful at best."

"Usually?" she asked, again picking up on some reluctance in his voice and body language. "When haven't they?"

"The only cop funerals I've seen go ignored and unannounced were suicides and bad off-duty situations."

"It wasn't either of those," Munch said firmly. "Especially not suicide. He was Catholic. A good Catholic."

"Of course he was," St. John said. "To the best of my knowledge, it wasn't anything like suicide. He died fighting."

Several hours later, Munch had to get out of the house. She walked to the market and bought a quart of milk. Caroline St. John took Asia to school at 8:30 A.M. They had decided not to tell Asia until after school. Let the kid have a few more hours of blissful ignorance. This also gave Munch a little more time to come to terms with it all before having to explain the unexplainable to her daughter.

Remember the Challenger, honey, and how that schoolteacher died? This is much worse.

The world had changed. People conducted their business, gave up their money for services and products, grew impatient with traffic, cared about the color of their houses and how much water the neighbor used to water his lawn.

Munch had a secret. None of that shit mattered. It was oddly freeing. She even felt superior, maybe enlightened was more like it. The problem with this newfound wisdom was that when nothing mattered, nothing mattered.

29

When she got back from the store, Munch changed out of her Texaco uniform to go visit Rico's father. She put on a pair of Levi's, T-shirt, and tennis shoes.

Fernando Chacón had a small house in Lawndale. He lived there with his son Cruz. Cruz was thirty-three, but would always need help for the simplest of life functions. His fingers and toes curled spastically inward and he moved in lurching steps. He had the mental capacity of a toddler and spoke in a minimal language only understood by his immediate family. An older Mexican woman came in five days a week to cook and clean for the two men since Rico's mother had died.

Like a toddler, Cruz needed constant supervision. When the family had lived in San Ysidro, the border town in California opposite Tijuana, Cruz had once gotten out of the house and walked across the footbridge connecting the two countries.

Rico and his mother had had to use connections and bribes to locate the missing man in a Tijuana jail and negotiate his release. Rico had hated the way they did business in his country of birth, but knew how to operate within its corrupt system.

Fernando was sitting in his garage when Munch pulled up. He was wearing lace-up boots, thick canvas pants, and a matching long-sleeved shirt. A dark oval of unbleached fabric over the pocket remained where a name tag had once been stitched. He, like Munch, had opted for clothes that gave him maximum mobility.

Soon, she knew, he would be breaking out his black suit and dusting off his lone pair of shiny black loafers.

Fernando kept a card table set up in his garage with several folding chairs. A heavy bag hung in one corner and the big round plastic dial of a chocolate-brown Admiral radio was tuned to a Spanish-language talk station. Rico used to call the setup his dad's fort. When Rico's mom was alive, Fernando purposely smoked big smelly cigars to ensure her exclusion.

Today there was a bottle of mescal on the table and two other middle-aged Mexican men sat with him gripping jelly-jar glasses in their callused hands. Their faces were brown and deeply lined, their bodies solid with muscle and unstooped by age, their otherwise dark hair gray-streaked. The men didn't smile when she approached. Fernando's expression under the brim of his Dodgers cap was particularly grim. Munch didn't feel he'd ever approved of her. She supposed he thought that his son needed and deserved a more traditional wife.

She wondered if he also blamed her.

Fernando lumbered to his feet. He seemed to have aged twenty years overnight. She hesitated at the entrance of the garage, willing to accept whatever recriminations he had for her. He crossed the cement floor to meet her. His arms raised up. She flinched. He pulled her to him and hugged her tightly. Munch buried her face in his shoulder. She tried to cry quietly and hold back the racking sobs. This man who would have been her father-in-law, this poor man who must deal with the loss of his wife and son, didn't need a hysterical woman on his hands.

After a too-short moment, Fernando released her. She instantly missed the feel of his rough shirt against her cheek. The moment of comfort was as surprising as it was brief.

A Gran Torino pulled up to the curb behind Munch's GTO. Two white men in suits got out. The flashing of their badges was redundant.

"Here we go," Munch said.

Fernando grunted and put a hand on her shoulder. For him the gesture was as eloquent as any crafted speech.

"I'm looking for Fernando Chacón," the cop who had been the passenger said.

"You found him," Fernando said.

"I'm Detective Martin Grimes, this is my partner Phil Bayless. Can we go somewhere private to talk?" Both cops were gladiator-type specimens. White, six feet tall, with requisite cop mustaches. Obviously, Munch thought, they had joined the force before affirmative-action mandates had tilted the requirement scales.

Fernando stood tall and squared off. "I already know my son is dead."

"We just have some questions, sir," Bayless said.

"Can I see your identification again?" Munch asked.

"And who are you?" Grimes asked, obviously annoyed at having his authority questioned.

"Miranda Mancini," Munch said, also holding her ground.

The two cops looked at each other. "We have some questions for you, too," Bayless said.

He showed her his identification and gave her a business card. Bayless was with Internal Affairs. Playing the memory association game in her head, Munch instantly dubbed the two Grimy and Ball-less.

"Ask me anything you want," she said.

Bayless took her aside and pulled out a notebook. "So what do your friends call you?"

She studied him dry-eyed for a second before answering. "Munch."

"How long had you and Detective Chacón been seeing each other?"

"About a year and a half. You know we were planning on getting married, right?"

Bayless looked up from his notebook. He seemed ill at ease, or maybe he was just the nervous sort.

"I'm sorry," he said, and those words sounded genuine enough. "Had you combined households?"

"We were going to buy a house, but I canceled the deal."

"When?"

"This morning. Right after I got the news Rico had died."

Bayless nodded, as if the timing made sense, but then asked, "Why?"

"Why?" Munch wondered if this was some dumb-cop routine, but decided to play it straight with the guy. "Because it was supposed to be our house and I couldn't afford it alone."

"Was Chacón supplying the money?"

"We both were."

"And did you have a joint bank account?"

"No."

"Did Chacón get any mail at your house or perhaps at a PO box you knew about?"

She felt her hackles rising. What were they insinuating? "I'm not even sure what kind of stamps he preferred. You want to tell me what any of this has to do with anything?"

"If you would just answer the questions to the best of your knowledge, we'll determine that when all the facts are in."

"He was a good and moral man."

Bayless nodded.

Munch pointed at his open notebook. "Write that down."

"Would you say he was loyal?" Bayless asked.

"Completely," Munch said, deciding to limit her answers to one-word responses. It wasn't looking like she and old Ball-less here were going to be new best friends after all.

"And you characterize him as an honest man?"

A two-word response came to mind, but she didn't want to come off defensive. "Yes, I would."

"How far would he go to protect a loved one?"

Munch blinked. "How is anyone supposed to know the answer to that? I'd step in front of a train for my kid. Is that the kind of protection you're talking about? Who was in trouble, and why?"

Bayless waved aside her question as if he were swatting a gnat. "When was the last time you saw him?"

"A week ago."

"Was that unusual?"

"We made time together when we could. It was never enough."

She looked over and caught Fernando's eye. He had crossed his arms over his chest and was shaking his head no to Grimes's questions. Soon he would lose his English.

"Who's handling the criminal investigation?" she asked Bayless. She wanted to add, *Not this bullshit witch-hunt;* but she didn't. It was too early to burn this guy as a possible resource.

"They'll be contacting you in due course."

"Then I should probably get home."

"Just one more question," he said. "If you remember anything else, or if something comes up in the future that doesn't make sense, would you give me a call?"

"The man I loved is dead. How is anything supposed to make sense?"

"Maybe that's something we can figure out together."

"Yeah, sure. You and me. What a team we'll make."

Bayless had the grace to look uncomfortable. Munch felt an unwilling response of empathy for him. Since she'd been promoted to service manager at her gas station, there had been more times than she cared to count where she'd been an asshole for the sake of the business. And not always to the people who deserved it.

After the IA cops left, Munch stood on the sidewalk with Fernando.

"What's going on?" she asked. "No one has even told me how it happened."

"He was shot. Many times." Fernando's mouth turned down from the bitterness of the news. "This is all I know."

Munch shut her eyes against the image of ripped flesh and shattered bone. "Have you spoken to Angelica?" she asked, although what she was really wondering about was if Fernando had turned to

Rico's first wife, Sylvia. Was Munch jealous even now? She couldn't tell and didn't want to examine her feelings too closely. She already had enough to hate herself for.

"Yes, they are coming over later with the rest of the family."

She was glad he wasn't going to be alone. That's what was important. "Can I use your phone?"

"Of course, *hija*." Daughter. He'd never used that endearment with her before.

She passed through the darkness of the garage quickly. Her grief had settled in her throat, making it difficult to swallow. Cruz was in the living room, standing as she often saw him with his forehead pressed against the bronze-veined mirrored wall, head bent down so that he could see the reflections. He turned to her, startled by the noise, and she saw that his face was wet with tears. She put a hand on his shoulder and said, "We'll get through this."

She used the kitchen phone to call Ellen.

"Hi," was all she said.

"What's wrong?" Ellen immediately asked.

"It's Rico."

"What's he gone and done?"

"He died."

"He what? Oh, shit. No way. Oh, sugar, I'm sorry. Damn. How? When?"

"Some kind of shoot-out, I think; they haven't told me much or with whom. Listen, I need your help."

"Anything," Ellen said without hesitation. She knew Munch well enough to know she'd only ask once.

"I need to go over to . . ." Munch hesitated. Was it far-fetched to think that the phone might be bugged? "The mall. I'm going to need a new outfit."

"Where are you now? You want me to pick you up?"

"Yeah, meet me at the Brentwood Country Mart. We can leave my car there."

"Should I bring anything?" she asked.

"You might want to wear comfortable shoes."

The Brentwood Country Mart was a grouping of faux barn buildings on the corner of Twenty-sixth and San Vincente. The mini-mall had all the neighborhood essentials, including a hardware store and a market. If people didn't care about paying top dollar, they could get film developed, prescriptions filled, and buy toys. There were also a world-class deli, a central courtyard where shoppers could nosh on rotisserie chicken, and several boutiques that sold the other necessities, such as three-hundred-dollar beaded evening bags and handmade Italian loafers.

Munch parked among the Mercedes and Cadillacs. Ellen was already there waiting, although it took Munch a moment to recognize her friend in long black beaded braids, fringed buckskin jacket, and matching moccasins. Ellen walked over while Munch locked her car.

Munch took a closer look. "I like the eyes."

Ellen batted her long lashes. "Honey amber. I just got them."

They embraced. Munch drank in the body contact, felt nourished by it, and—in another first for them—let Ellen break it off first.

Ellen brushed a lock of hair from Munch's face and tucked it behind one ear. "How you doing, kid?"

Munch shrugged. She didn't like to lie or complain, and that left little to say.

Ellen put a protective arm around Munch's shoulders. "Now, Miss I-Need-a-New-Outfit, where are we *really* going?"

"Rico's house. I want to look around. Something stinks."

CHAPTER SIX

RICO'S HOUSE WAS IN SANTA MONICA CANYON. THE garage faced the street and the front door was actually on the side of the house, facing the next-door neighbor's side fence. Munch had Ellen park a few doors down the street.

"Honk twice if you see anyone coming." Munch looked up and down the block as she got out of Ellen's Camaro.

"You want me to create a diversion or something?"

Munch had to smile. Creating diversions was one of Ellen's specialities. She didn't even need a reason and it often involved lifting her blouse to her chin. "Let's play it by ear, Pocahontas."

Munch used her key to let herself in. Once inside the door, she turned off the alarm. She looked for signs that someone else had been there, but couldn't detect any. Neither the police nor the coroner had put their seal on the door. Not that a piece of gummed paper would have stopped her.

The two-bedroom beach bungalow was definitely a bachelor's pad. No dining room. A Pac-Man video game served as a small table. The kitchen was open, defined from the living room by a high counter. On the occasions that they had eaten meals there, she and Rico had perched on the barstools side by side.

His stereo system was top of the line, Harman Kardon, and every room boasted a television suspended by brackets from the ceiling. Over the large overstuffed leather sofa hung a framed fight poster advertising last year's bout between "Boom Boom" Mancini and

Bobby Chacón. Mancini had won by a unanimous decision. Munch wondered if anyone would object to her keeping the poster.

The focal point of the master bedroom was the king-size bed. The spread was pulled hastily across lumpy sheets. She lay down on his side and rested her head on his pillow. He always took the side closest to the door. He wanted to be the first line of defense against an intruder.

How far would he go to protect someone he loved? Where had that question come from? Was it a fishing expedition, or had Bayless been trying one of those cop head trips on her? Sometimes they were able to finesse a confession by providing the guilty person an out. People naturally wanted to tell the truth. Giving them a logical excuse for their actions made honesty that much easier.

She studied her image in the mirrored closet door, curious to see if her grief showed in her face. So far she looked the same. The dark circles under her hazel eyes would come later, after the long sleepless nights. There was an odd sort of comfort in her melancholy; maybe it was just the return to familiar territory.

Rico's brown corduroy coat sleeve prevented the sliding closet door from closing all the way. It was the jacket he had worn the day they ran across the gang-banger with the pit bull. She pulled the coat off its hanger and put it on. She had to fold back the cuffs three times before the sleeves ended at her wrists.

She slid the door open and stared at the costumes of his undercover work mixed with his dress clothes. A clear plastic dry cleaner's bag shrouded a blue uniform with its patches and rank insignia.

Last year, she had helped Ellen pick out the clothes to bury her parents—all three of them, counting her stepfather. The Colonel, Ellen's long-lost dad, had left instructions to be buried in his uniform. Rico would have wished the same thing. He told her once that being a cop was the only career he'd wanted since high school.

Yeah, being buried in his uniform was one of those traditions he probably would have dug.

A chill came over her and she pulled the jacket tight around her. She went into the second bedroom, the one Rico used as his office.

On the top of his desk was a file folder with "Wedding" written on the tab. She opened it to find menu selections and a sheet of lined yellow paper torn from a legal pad. It was a working copy of the wedding-guest list. How convenient to have a roll call of all the same people she would be inviting to the funeral. Rico had also torn out a glossy magazine ad of a tuxedo with a ruffled shirt. It made her think of the fuzzy dice hanging from the rearview mirror of his low rider. Sometimes the guy was such a beaner, it made her want to cringe.

Not now. Now all his idiosyncrasies and flaws would be forgotten or remembered with affection.

She lifted the desk blotter and found a United Airlines envelope. Inside were two airline tickets to Hawaii. Under that envelope were two aged Hallmark greeting cards. The printed cards were gushy miss-you, love-you types and signed by two different women: a Victoria and a Christina. The names meant nothing to her. Munch wished the bitches had had the consideration to date their declarations. Now she'd have to wonder.

The airline tickets were in the names of Mr. and Mrs. Enrique Chacón. She put the tickets back. They were too sad to contemplate, and she didn't want anyone to accuse her later of taking anything of monetary value.

The top right-hand drawer of the desk yielded pictures. She started to select a few and then stopped. Maybe his daughter or his father and brothers would want to have first pick. The bottom drawer also had pictures in it, or rather a single large manila envelope full of snapshots.

She pulled them out and fanned them across the desktop, wondering why these weren't with the others. She imagined there would be many unanswered questions in the days to come.

The pictures were of various family members. Fernando and Cruz in the driveway of the Lawndale house. Rico's ex, Sylvia, and daughter, Angelica, taken as they got in a car outside their house in Los Feliz. This dated them. The move to the Los Feliz house had been two months ago.

Other photos were of Rico's brothers and their families. Several were shots of older Mexican men and women who might have been aunts and uncles. Judging by the unpaved roads and the laundry drying on the bushes, these were taken in Mexico.

There were also pictures of her and Asia, even one of Jasper. She looked hard at the photos, trying to remember the occasion. She wasn't smiling for the photograph and neither was Asia, which was really odd. The kid was such a ham.

Munch went back over the other pictures and noticed that none of the subjects had smiled for the camera or even looked directly at it.

Two honks broke through her thoughts. Ellen's signal.

Munch pocketed Rico's address book and put the pictures back where she had found them. She made for the bathroom off the hallway between the two bedrooms. It had a door that led to the backyard. Rico's brush was on the sink counter, lying there as if he had just put it down. Long strands of black hair trailed from the bristles. She couldn't help but notice how much longer they were than Rico's own hair as she let herself out the back door, but she had no time to ponder their source now.

She came around the side of the house, crouching low so as to be concealed by the retaining wall that separated the pool from the steep bank of ivy. She thought briefly of the rats that lived in the undergrowth as she headed toward the far side of the garage.

Rolls of chain link and odd-sized lengths of two-by-fours were piled helter-skelter against the outer garage wall. Weeds grew in between the metal and wood. One misstep could bring the mess tumbling apart noisily. The last thing she wanted was for whoever had caused Ellen to give the warning signal to catch her.

Car doors slammed one after the other and Munch hazarded a peek around the edge of the garage wall.

A van and a car had pulled into the driveway. The van, according to the lettering on the side, belonged to a locksmith, the car was a blue Ford Mustang, a Shelby. She'd locked the front door after herself, but the alarm was still turned off. *Shit*. She'd made it easy for them. Two men got out of the car—one was a longhair, the other clean-cut—and waited for the locksmith. They all headed for the front door and out of her line of vision. The locksmith carried his toolbox, the two other men carried cardboard file boxes. The boxes were empty, judging by the way they handled them. She waited until the three men had turned the corner, then made a break up the driveway.

Ellen started the engine when Munch was almost to the passenger door. "Those were cops, right?"

"I guess," Munch said. "Pretty nice ride for a cop. Those Shelby Mustangs go for three times the rate of a regular Mustang, and those aren't cheap to begin with."

"They took the mail right out of the box." Ellen swung into the lane with a wide U-turn, taking them past the house again. "Isn't that a federal crime, to mess with the mail?"

"A lot of rules don't apply to cops." Munch wished *she'd* thought to check Rico's mail. "Go slow," she told Ellen as they passed the house. The locksmith was working on the dead bolt. The other two were joking with each other as they waited. She would have loved to stay and give them the evil eye, but it was time to pick up Asia at school and explain why their lives had changed.

CHAPTER SEVEN

ELLEN DROVE MUNCH BACK TO HER CAR. MUNCH WAS quiet on the trip over, staring out the window, contemplating a sad future. She had told Cruz that they would get through this, but only because she knew he wouldn't ask how.

Asia's school bus would be dropping her off soon. Ellen offered to come along, Munch didn't hesitate to accept. She'd done her share for Ellen in the past and then some. Ellen made the favor easier by offering. She knew how difficult it was to ask for help, how bad it felt when someone told you no after you'd screwed your courage up and asked.

Telling Asia was going to be rough. She understood much better than most kids what death meant and how forever it was.

When Munch's mom had died, she was only a year older than Asia was now. Walking around school after that, it was as if a force field projected from her. She was the kid whose mom had died. That scary, unknown prospect kept everyone from coming too close. Now Munch understood that the isolation she'd felt hadn't been intended to hurt her. The teachers had probably been worried about saying the wrong thing. Or maybe they thought by not bringing the subject up, Munch wouldn't think about her orphan status so much.

None of Munch's young friends could help her either. None of them had lost a parent, and most of them had two to begin with. Munch quickly learned that people's sympathy had limits. Most people who asked how she was had only wanted to hear, "Fine."

That was still true.

When adults took the risk of addressing her situation, it was to praise her for being tough, for moving on. She had begun getting in fistfights at school, her grades should have slipped, but the teachers went easy on her. Not that there had been anyone in her life to read or miss the signs.

Sometimes, young Munch slipped away from school in the middle of the day. Once, while rambling along in an alley, she came across a gate strung with barbed wire. Not sure how serious she was, she ran her wrists across the sharp wire spikes. Enough to scratch the skin. The next time, she drew blood. At ten years old, she didn't know what she was trying to accomplish. She was staying with doper friends of her mom who barely noticed when she came and went, never asked her to account for her time, and let her eat whatever she could scrounge.

When she got home that day, she didn't wash the wounds and wore short sleeves to school the next morning. No one asked about the lines of scabs crisscrossing her wrists. Her invisibility continued, as did her survival/destruction instincts.

When Flower George stepped up to be Munch's dad, she was open to suggestion. The same had been true when she started using. Strange as she knew it might sound, drugs had saved her or at least given her a greater purpose. Then the booze and narcotics had joined the pantheon of her life's love/hate relationships. Her life was full of yins and yangs, and never short of extreme.

Even now, twenty years later, Munch had to remind herself that suicide wasn't an option, not if she was buying into the theory that there was a Higher Power with a plan. Some days it was harder than others.

"What are you thinking about?" Ellen asked.

"My mom. I wish you could have met her."

"Me, too," Ellen said as they pulled into the gas station to wait for the school bus. "How are you going to tell Asia about this?"

"I thought we'd go to a park, maybe that one on Alla Road, near the Marina Freeway."

They watched the traffic go by. Munch wondered where everyone was going and who would make it.

"Who told you when your mom died?" Ellen asked.

"I was in school when it happened. Miss Hyde's class, fourth grade." Munch remembered Miss Hyde vividly. She wore her black hair in a beehive, painted her unsmiling lips with dark red lipstick, wore her dresses mid-calf, and encased her feet in sheer stockings and black patent leather pumps. Miss Hyde was the polar opposite of Munch's beatnik, free-spirited mother Gloria.

Mama wore her hair long and free, didn't believe there was such a thing as too much black eyeliner, and wouldn't be caught in a skirt and heels if her life depended on it.

The mother Munch remembered (and those memories grew more intangible with each passing year) dressed in flowing gypsy clothes, smoked like a diesel truck, and didn't believe in bras, war, or marriage. She also loved her drugs and died on a stranger's couch, choking on her own vomit with her shirt on inside out. If she had been wearing panties, they never surfaced.

Flower George was not above using those small horrid details of her mother's passing to his advantage. Say, for instance, if he needed her unbridled tears to perpetrate one of his scams. That device stopped working after the first few times. Then Munch was immune to his words and he had to figure other ways for her to earn her keep.

Munch stared out the window, replaying the moment she had learned she was a motherless child. "Miss Hyde told me the principal wanted to see me, but she wouldn't say why. She called me honey and put her hand on my shoulder. I should have known then something was up. She was never nice to anyone."

Ellen nodded. "Yeah, that's always a big giveaway, when people are suddenly too friendly."

"I went to see the principal. She was a big, bosomy woman. Old.

Old to us then, like she could be someone's grandma. She was probably in her forties. Mrs. Adams. The secretary led me into Mrs. Adams's private office, then closed the door behind her, leaving just the two of us alone. Mrs. Adams was standing by her desk. 'Miranda,' she said, 'I have some sad news.' "

"Sad news?" Ellen slammed her palm to her forehead. "She actually said that?"

"Well, she was right. It was pretty fucking sad. What should she have done? Line up all the kids at assembly and announce, 'Everyone with a living mother take a step forward. Not so fast, Miranda.' "

Ellen laughed, a privilege of being a member of the dead mothers club.

"She just came right out with it and said, 'Your mother has died. I'm sorry.' Then she held her arms out to me and I realized I was supposed to let her hug me, so I ran into her big chest and buried my face there."

"You think it made her feel better?" Ellen asked.

"Probably. I was ten. I sure didn't get what death meant. How final it was. I had to take my cues from the grown-ups around me."

"I feel like I'm still doing that," Ellen said.

"I hear you."

"The more you know, the more you know you don't know."

"You got that right, babycakes." Munch looked into the near future, the next hour. That was as far as she cared to go for the moment. "Yep, that's best. That's how I'll do it. Just come right out with it."

"Hug her first."

"I don't know about that. I don't want her scared of my hugs."

Ellen nodded. "Like they're harbingers of bad news."

Munch sputtered a surprised laugh and looked at her friend as if she had just begun speaking in tongues.

"What?" Ellen said. "I read more than the *National Enquirer*."

"Of course." No doubt during one of her stays at the University of Corrections.

Asia's bus pulled up, a moment later she skipped off. When she saw her mom and Aunt Ellen, she smiled and waved. Munch would have given the world not to have to ruin this day.

They stopped at Baskin-Robbins and got ice cream cones. Asia had vanilla with sprinkles. Munch got a scoop of pralines and cream. Ellen had rocky road. Munch waited until they were all seated on a bench overlooking the sandbox.

Munch's ice cream had pretty much melted down her hand. Asia and Ellen were taking the last bites out of their cones. Ellen looked at Munch, probably wondering when Munch would feel the time was right.

Munch threw away her cone, took a sip of cold water from the drinking fountain and rinsed her hand. She allowed herself to be captivated momentarily by the water swirling down the drain. Sometimes life was best experienced one freeze frame at a time.

The nuns at Asia's school would tell her that the angels had taken Rico home. Or that her deceased loved one was looking at the face of God. Munch couldn't choke those words out. Those sentiments required acceptance, a reconciliation with laws of fate, surrender. She wasn't anywhere near that state of grace, more like a state of astonishment that something like this had happened. That, with all her clean living and good deeds and correct moral choices, Whoever was in charge had allowed this shit.

Goddamn it, it wasn't fair.

Fair. Listen to her. Munch knew better than to expect fair. But she was not going to explain to her daughter why it made any kind of sense. Because it didn't. It just didn't.

She rejoined Asia and Ellen by the swing set. She brushed back Asia's brown curls from her eyes and sat down beside her. "Honey, I have some sad news."

Asia was more quizzical than apprehensive.

Munch looked at Ellen, then back at her daughter. "Some really, really terrible news."

She had Asia's full attention.

"You know how Mace St. John came over real early this morning?"

Asia poked a small finger up her nose, nodding as she itched or picked or whatever she'd suddenly gotten so intent on doing.

"He found out that something happened to Rico and wanted to tell me in person. I don't know how and I don't know why yet, but Rico got killed. He's dead."

"No he's not," Asia said.

Munch nodded slowly. She didn't want to keep saying the words.

Terror flashed unmistakably before the tears burbled from Asia's brown eyes. She looked to her mother for . . . what? For something. Munch knew she was supposed to supply more to the moment, but she had nothing. She was screwing this up.

"He loved you both very much," Ellen said.

"Then why did he have to die?" Asia asked. "Is this going to happen every time now?"

Munch couldn't speak. Her whole body ached and she felt tired, the act of keeping her eyes open taxed her. How nice it would be to curl up and sleep.

Asia folded her arms across her chest. "I wish he was here."

Munch unwrapped her daughter's arms and fit them around her neck. She hugged her daughter to her as if she were drowning. "Me, too, kiddo. Me, too."

As Asia sobbed into her chest, Munch realized that this was going to be like kicking an addiction. Unable to take comfort in the only thing that could give her comfort. If Rico weren't dead, he would be the person she would call about this. It was his shoulder she yearned to cry on. But that wasn't going to happen, was it? They would have to make do with what was left.

The first night . . .

Munch moved to what had been Rico's side of her bed; his scent was on the pillow. A poor substitute. She got up, stripped the bed, and washed the sheets and pillowcases with extra bleach. He no longer had a side. He was gone and she needed to get used to that.

Sometime in the middle of the night, Asia climbed in bed with Munch. Munch pretended she was asleep. Jasper groaned once, then settled his head on Munch's leg. Asia's little hand reached over to pat Munch's back. Munch waited until they were both snoring, then let her tears fall silently into the pillowcase. She drew a deep breath and felt it shudder her chest on exhale, as if everything inside were hanging in tatters. She'd never felt so fragile before and she didn't like it. She had to be strong for all of them.

CHAPTER EIGHT

THE DAY AFTER . . .

At the IA officer's request, Munch went to see Bayless. They made an appointment to meet at his Parker Center office in downtown Los Angeles at ten that morning.

She gave her name at the desk and then waited by the potted palms.

Two minutes later, Bayless stepped off one of the elevators. The cop at the front desk gave her a visitor's badge to pin to her shirt. Bayless escorted her upstairs. It was her first time on the sixth floor. He offered her coffee. She declined. He poured himself a cup from the Mr. Coffee machine on top of his filing cabinet.

She noticed the thick gold wedding band on his finger. "How long have you been married?"

"Three years."

"Not your first, I take it."

"No, no, no." He chuckled as he spoke, as if she had stumbled on a source of amusement for him.

"I've never been married," Munch said.

"What about your daughter's father?"

She looked at him a moment, surprised that he knew she had a daughter. Maybe it was to her advantage. "He's dead, so's Asia's birth mom. It's been her and me since she was a little baby."

Bayless nodded, taking it in. Munch knew full well why she was telling him all this. To make herself more real to him. So he wouldn't be able to brush her or her questions aside so easily.

She looked at the backs of the picture frames on his desk. He kept the faces of his loved ones pointed toward him. She wondered about that. Not on a shelf for the world's benefit, proof that he had people, but private and only for him. She wasn't sure if she liked that or not. "You got kids?"

"Oh, yeah."

"How many?"

He looked up and to his left. Munch wondered if he needed a moment to count them all. "Two boys. Two girls. And a girl."

"So three girls." Munch wondered if the guy was stupid, pretending to be stupid, or if the third daughter had arrived much later. Maybe he'd been used to having two daughters for more years and with a previous wife. She noticed a pair of tiny bronzed shoes weighing down a stack of closed files. "How old is the baby?"

"Almost four." He took a sip of his coffee, then placed the mug carefully on an envelope, nearly positioning it perfectly inside a previous ringed brown stain. "You're not here to talk about me."

She watched the steam rise from the windowsill. It had been cold and wet that morning, but now the sun was breaking through. She wondered if, four years down the road, if someone asked her if she had ever been married, would she need to pause a moment and think about it? Would she look vaguely skyward and say something like, *I was engaged once, briefly*.

"Ms. Mancini?"

"What?"

"What do you think happened to Detective Chacón?"

"I sent him to his death."

He folded his hands in front of him. "How did you do that?"

"I was hoping you could help me figure that out."

"If you're serious, there are ways you can help."

"Whatever it takes."

"Fine," he said. "Tell me what you know."

So this was to be another variation of the old let's-share-everything game. You go first. According to the rules she'd been raised with, players never shared everything they had on the first round. True players never gave away everything.

"He was trying to save me." That's not how she had wanted to start. She didn't consider herself a person who needed constant rescue. She began again with the words that launched so many stories: "There's this guy."

Bayless clicked his pen open. "This guy have a name?"

"Peter Donner. Goes by Petey. He's a biker, a one-percenter."

Bayless looked up from his notebook, his expression nonplussed.

"You know," she explained, "ninety-nine percent of the population are citizens, one percent are outlaws. Anyhow, this Petey guy is the president of the Satan's Pride." She waited for Bayless to write the cop code for asshole, but he only wrote: "Donner, Peter."

"Go on."

"Years ago"—she swept her hand to the side to indicate just how far in the past this all was—"I used to hang with the Satan's Pride. The Venice chapter. Anyway, you know how bad they treat women, right?"

Bayless held his pen over his pad, waiting to write something novel. Apparently the misogynistic tendencies of outlaw bikers wasn't breaking news.

Munch nodded. She needed just to come right out with it, stop worrying about how it was all going to sound to someone who didn't know her better. "Okay. I found out that Petey is looking to revitalize the local chapter. He offered a patch to the first guy who brought me in."

"Why you?"

"About nine years ago, I brought the club down. Not single-handedly, but if I'd kept my mouth shut and died like I was supposed to, they'd still be active in these parts. I feel just terrible about it."

Bayless smirked. "Nine years ago did you work with the police?"

"I told them what I knew about some women getting killed; they put the rest together."

"Was Rico Chacón part of all that?"

"No. I hadn't met him yet." She considered telling Bayless about Mace St. John and how they'd saved each other, figuratively and literally, then decided that that would be something that might help her more later. Sometimes it was better to let people think you had no friends or pull and see how they treated you. "Rico found out about Petey's threat." Munch didn't say how, well aware that she was treading some muddy waters. She was pretty certain that Rico had crossed a few lines to help her more than once. Bringing that up now might be all the proof Bayless needed to rule against Rico. "Rico told me he'd handle it. Now he's dead."

"So you think this Peter Donner killed Rico?"

"I have no idea. All Rico's dad said was that Rico was shot to death. Do you have suspects or witnesses or anything?"

"I can't discuss an ongoing investigation."

"What the hell have we been doing, then?"

"Let me check with my sergeant and I'll see how much I can tell you. Do you still communicate with any of your biker friends?"

"Never on purpose. I'm sure you've read my jacket. That should tell my story. I travel in different circles now. There's not a lot of chopper traffic in Brentwood."

"Sounds like it's been a while since you hit the bar scene."

"I don't even live in the same universe anymore."

Munch left Bayless and drove over to Fernando's house. Cars and pickup trucks lined both sides of the street. Mourners spilled into the front lawn and sidewalk, mostly men. The women, Munch knew, would be inside cooking. Rico's ex, Sylvia, wouldn't miss this opportunity to insert herself into the middle of the action.

Munch found Madame Ex at the stove adding spices to a large cauldron of red sauce. A red bandanna tamed her kinky hair. Her black skin shone with sweat.

Munch forced a smile on to her face. "You want some help?"

Sylvia, grimacing, looked Munch up and down. "No. You'll just be in the way."

Granted, cooking wasn't Munch's thing, but that wasn't the issue. "I'm going to be a part of this. You might as well get used to that."

"Fine. The funeral is Saturday. We'll be coming back here after."

"Is this house going to be big enough?"

"It will just be family." Sylvia again gave Munch a look usually reserved for nasty jobs that couldn't be put off indefinitely, such as cleaning toilet bowls. "We'll manage."

"I've seen cop funerals before. They're huge. They close down intersections for the procession."

"This funeral is going to be small," Sylvia said. "Fernando will barely be able to afford a nice casket. The costs to bury someone in the States are unbelievable."

"That should be the least of his worries. I'm pretty sure the city has some kind of fund for this. I'll make some calls and find out."

"Oh, yes," Sylvia's tone was acidic. It went nicely with her facial expression. "There are many funds. The federal government is supposed to pay the family five hundred thousand dollars when a police office is killed in the line of duty. A man told us this morning that Rico's family is not eligible to collect. Now the city's risk management department is holding back his benefits, his pension, everything."

"And not even footing the bill for the funeral?"

"We don't want their empty gestures."

Munch realized her mouth was hanging open. She didn't understand. "No pension?"

"That's right, nothing for his own daughter." Sylvia looked past the Formica kitchen table to where Angelica sat in the backyard listlessly petting the family's chow. "We will continue to suffer." Her tone seemed to imply this would be happening long after Munch had gotten over it all.

Munch wanted to shake the woman. Did Sylvia think Munch's grief wasn't measuring up? "Fernando told me Rico was killed in a shoot-out. How much more in the line of duty could he have been?"

"According to his commander, he was not where he was supposed to be. *Puto*." Sylvia attacked a pile of cilantro with vengeance. "They said he was dirty. A dirty cop."

"Bullshit. Who says?"

"The narcos who shot him."

Munch felt a shift in her equilibrium. The humming in her ears was so intense, she wasn't sure she would be able to hear anything else. "Wait a minute. You're saying he was shot by other cops? It must have been a case of mistaken identity, an accident. One of those friendly-fire scenarios. He's been working undercover."

"Was he?" Sylvia turned on Munch, punctuating her words with unmasked contempt.

"You can't possibly believe he was crooked. Did you know him at all?" Munch took a step back and pulled her hands out of her pockets. It was with some effort that she didn't ball her fists. "I want to talk to these cops."

"Go ahead," Sylvia said. "Maybe they'll shoot you, too."

Munch might beat herself up all day long, but there was a limit to how much shit she'd take from anyone else. Hell, it wasn't as if she broke up the family or anything. Rico and Sylvia had been split up for years when Munch and he got together. Before she said or did anything she might regret, Munch left Madame Head-Up-Her-Ass Ex and went out into the backyard. Angelica looked skinnier than ever. Her Levi's-clad legs were little more than bones and her shoulders slumped as if she were exhausted.

One cooked while the other starved. Welcome to America.

Munch would have liked to hug the girl, but she knew from past experience that Angelica didn't like being touched. Angelica didn't seem to like much of anything.

"Your mom is making enough to feed an army in there."

Angelica's eyes were brown like Rico's, but held no shine. "Yeah?"

"Smells good."

Angelica twisted her back as if trying to loosen a kink, as if her muscles were fifty years old instead of fifteen. Munch wanted to hold the kid down and pump nourishment into her.

"If you need anything, call me. Okay?"

"I'm fine," Angelica said.

"I didn't ask how you were. You don't have to lie to me."

"I don't have to talk to you either."

"Only if you want to. I can be a good friend. Remember that."

Munch drove home. First she stopped at the market and called St. John from the pay phone there. She filled him in on the latest twists. "I know you didn't love Rico, but there is no way he was bad. This is some horrible mistake."

"I've seen the report," St. John said. "Rico was trading fire with the task force. If he wasn't playing for the other team, I don't know what the explanation is."

"So when you said IA investigates all officer-involved shootings—"

"I'm sorry. I didn't mean to withhold from you, but I thought it would be better if your surprise at the circumstances of his death was genuine."

"It was that." Munch rubbed her throat, trying to loosen the ache there. "Can you set up a meeting with them for me?"

"With who?"

"The task force cops."

"I don't want you involved with these guys. Narcs are ego-driven cowboys. All they care about is putting powder on the table and bodies in jail."

"But Rico was a brother cop."

"Don't count on that to help you. The word is that he was assisting in a prison break of some Mexican nationals, some narcotraffickers."

"That doesn't make any sense. You can't believe that."

"We'll both have to wait until all the evidence comes in," he said.

"And how long will that take?" she asked.

"I need you to be patient. Don't even think about doing anything half-cocked."

"I won't."

He snorted into the phone as if he didn't believe her. "The best you can do is stay off their radar. They're gonna look at you and just try to figure how to use you. You make too much noise, and they'll find a hammer to hold over your head."

"Like what?"

"Either they'll think you're involved or they'll approach you to assist with their investigation and make sure you do whether you want to or not. It's not nice, but it's the way it is. They love it when a person of interest has a kid, gives them great leverage. They like threatening to put the kid in child services if the parents don't cooperate."

"You wouldn't let that happen."

"I'd fight like hell, but I might only be able to do so much."

"I hear what you're saying about these guys." *This way there be dragons*. "Can you give me their names at least?"

"Absolutely not."

"You want a couple more seconds to think about that? You sound a little on the fence."

"The best thing for you to do is get on with your life, let some time pass."

Munch looked up at her ceiling and rubbed her eyes. Her sinuses were filled with tear-diluted mucus and they burned. It was the same feeling she used to get as a kid when the waves would somersault her on to the ocean floor. Let time pass? Every hour was a week long. He didn't know what he was asking.

"Fine." She hung up without saying good-bye and picked up her TO DO list. She added: "narc's names."

CHAPTER NINE

MUNCH PULLED BAYLESS'S CARD FROM HER WALLET AND stared at it.

"Fuck 'em," she muttered to herself as she dialed.

"Bayless, Internal Investigations."

She had to clear her throat before she began. "This is Munch Mancini."

"What can I do for you?"

"Do you investigate *all* cop shootings?"

"Not every case crosses my desk."

"In Rico's case, which end are you looking at?"

"What do you mean?"

"According to his ex-wife, Rico Chacón was shot by other cops. Narcs. So are you looking at Rico as a shooter or as the guy who got shot?"

"This is not something we should discuss on the phone."

Munch's heartbeat quickened. He hadn't shut the door on her. "What are you saying?"

"Why don't you come to see me tomorrow? We'll kick this around a little."

"I'll be there at ten with my boots on."

Ellen offered to treat Munch and Asia to dinner. They went to a new restaurant in Santa Monica that offered organic Italian. Munch perused the menu, looking for something Asia would enjoy. She was feeling a few gnawing tugs of hunger for the first time that day. They seemed like a betrayal.

"Tofu pepperoni pizza," Ellen said, sounding outraged. She put her menu down. "Now that's just wrong."

Munch laughed out loud, feeling a touch of hysteria. She sensed that if she didn't keep it under control, she would be carried away on a cloud of mindless hilarity. Still, it felt good to laugh, even as it hurt a little, too. As if some shell were breaking apart inside her. She leaned over to Asia. "Let's get the Popeye pizza. Spinach and mozzarella."

"Okay, Mom. You're the boss."

Munch put a hand to Asia's forehead. "Are you feeling all right?"

Asia rolled her eyes until only the white showed. It was an expression she'd been making since before she could talk.

Munch let her hand linger and Asia didn't mind. How many more years did they have before Asia would get too hip, slick, and cool for her mom?

The waitress set water in front of them. "Are you guys ready?"

After they had placed their orders and the waitress had left, Munch put Asia's napkin in her lap. "I saw Angelica today."

"Was she sad?" Asia asked, a tiny crease appearing between her brown eyes.

"Yeah, although with her it's hard to tell."

"I know what you mean," Asia said. "She's a piece of work."

Munch choked on her water. "Where did you hear that expression?" Ellen raised both hands as if to plead her innocence.

"I get around," Asia said, affecting nonchalance.

Munch pushed her shoulder. "Cut that out. You're nine. Now act like it."

Asia stuck her tongue out.

"That's better."

"Who's Angelica?" Ellen asked.

"Rico's kid."

Asia raised her hand. "She was going to be my sister."

Munch pulled her daughter close to her. "She still can be. That doesn't have to change. In fact, she needs us now more than she knows. Rico would want us to be nice to her, don't you think?"

"Okay, but she better be nice back."

Munch tweaked Asia's nose. "Don't hold your breath. It might be up to us to make the first move."

Ellen sat up straighter and pulled her shoulders back. Some good-looking guy must have come into view. "Where did you see Rico's kid?"

"At the father's house. Rico's father. They're going to have everyone gather there after the services. Apparently it's just going to be family."

Ellen toyed with one of her dangling earrings. "Didn't Rico have a gang of brothers? And what about all his cop friends?"

"He had six brothers and a sister. Most of them will be there, but . . ."

Ellen turned too-green eyes on her and tilted her head in a silent question.

Munch lifted the napkin from Asia's lap and stood to let her out of the booth. "Asia, honey, go wash your hands."

"But—"

"Don't worry about mine."

Asia slumped her shoulders as she climbed out of the booth. "Ohh, all right, Mother."

Ellen smiled after her. "She's a trip and a half."

"Tell me about it." Munch rubbed her face with both hands. When she lowered them back to the table, Ellen was focused on her.

"What's going on?"

Munch glanced toward the bathroom door, knowing her time was limited. "I don't want a bunch of his co-workers at the service. I don't want to have to look at them. The cops are the ones who shot Rico. Some narc assholes."

Ellen's eyes swiveled to Munch's mouth as if she couldn't believe the words that had just spilled from it. "What? Was it some kind of accident? Did he know the guy?"

Everyone else in the restaurant was momentarily forgotten. Ellen's eyes filled with tears, matching Munch's own.

"I don't know. I'm trying to find out more." Munch spoke quickly, needing to get it all out before Asia returned. "Now a question has been raised about how honest a cop he was. His pension, death benefits, all that is being held back. Mace St. John said that none of his cop buddies are gonna want to get caught on the wrong side of whatever was going on."

"No way," Ellen said. "There's absolutely no fucking way that boy was on the take." She took a sip of water and dabbed her lips with her napkin. "No. He was into it—the whole law-and-order thing. I never got any other vibe from him."

Munch wiped at the tears leaking down her cheeks. She never knew she could cry so much. "You ask me, I think the narcs are just trying to cover their own asses. I'm not going to let them get away with it."

"Honey." Ellen reached over and patted Munch's hand. "This is me. Be real. If the cops want it to read a certain way, ain't a damned thing you can do about it."

"I'm not looking to change the world. I just want some answers."

"That's probably doable." She paused to dab at her lower lash line. The smudge of mascara there disappeared. "I'll help any way I can."

"I might need you to look after Asia for a few days."

"God, you must be desperate."

"I'm going to go see this guy tomorrow."

Asia returned to the table and the subject was changed.

On Wednesday morning, Munch drove downtown again to Parker Center, also referred to by those familiar with the building's multiple stories of green windows as The Glass House. The cop behind the counter smiled in recognition. Munch wondered at his open friendliness, then she had to remind herself that she no longer dressed like biker trash and had shed the pallor of addiction many years ago. It was still hard to get used to cops treating her like she wasn't prey or another scumbag to be wary of.

And sometimes vice versa.

Bayless was expecting her, but she was early. While she waited, she observed. The cop at the front desk had the patience of a saint, fielding all sorts of stupid questions. He was probably used to it.

She'd gone on a ride-along once—Rico had set it up when she expressed an interest. Mainly it had been for the novelty of riding in the front seat.

She'd felt a bit like a spy as she rode with a sheriff's deputy in East Los Angeles on his 6-A.M.-to-2-P.M. shift that Saturday. His name was Mike Savage. A lot of cops were named Mike, Officer Savage said. Saint Michael was the patron saint of cops.

The thing that had amazed her most about the day was the trivial, often ridiculous, bullshit people felt compelled to report. Lovers called the cops on exes; drunks in trailer parks called 911 to mediate beer distribution disputes; and, during the shift she shared, a disgruntled customer called the police when he felt an automotive shop had overcharged him for the removal of a cross-threaded head bolt. Savage called her over to help with that one. The owner of the garage had been Korean, the customer Hispanic, the car Japanese. After sorting out the language barrier, Munch had convinced the customer that the ten-dollar fee was fair. The whole business had used up twenty minutes of their patrol time.

When she and Deputy Mike stopped for lunch, he speculated aloud about what great legs she must have under the long pants she'd worn. This seemed to be another common thread among male cops. Total horn dogs.

Two plainclothes cops laughed about something as they walked past her now. Their suit jackets swung open to reveal the badges and guns clipped to their belts. She saw no black elastic mourning bands crisscrossing their shields. She wanted to stick out her foot and bring them crashing to their knees.

She looked down quickly, worried that her anger might transmit and bring unwanted attention to herself. Christ, she'd never ever seen these guys before. But, then again, what if they were the ones? What if they had already trimmed their long undercover hair, changed out of their grubby street clothes, and resumed their straight-cop lives?

She felt a strong compulsion to follow them, listen to their conversation, maybe shoot them if they needed it.

One of the elevators whooshed open and Bayless stepped into the lobby. Munch clipped on her visitor's badge and crossed onto his turf.

Parker Center had been built in the fifties and still had the original linoleum flooring. In some places the patterned top layer had worn through. The black-and-white photographs on the walls looked as if they'd hung there since the Korean War. The men in the pictures perched on the edge of desks and wore white shirts, thin ties, and hats. Everyone smoked. The women behind the typewriters, their legs crossed at the ankles, were all wearing mid-length dresses and heavy makeup. It was easy to tell the good guys back then. They were all white.

She realized she had taken the lead in the hallway and that Bayless was barely keeping up. She stopped to wait for him. What was she doing leading when she didn't know where they were going?

He pulled keys from his pocket. "Were you serious when you said you'd be willing to do anything to find out the truth?"

She almost smiled. This was going perfectly. "Absolutely."

"I can't say too much, but on reviewing the evidence, I'm forced to agree with you. Something doesn't add up."

They stopped in front of a frosted glass door that was slightly ajar. She assumed it was Bayless's office. Munch felt all her antennae stretch to their max. The whoosh of the air-conditioning, the creak of a chair in another office and the muted voice of one man, probably speaking on the phone—she recorded it all. Smells of burned coffee, ammonia, and a touch of mildew registered also. She brushed the wall with her fingertips, and stared again at the dead guys pictured there. It was all real. She was here. This was happening. "What can I do?"

Bayless's eyes stopped twitching for the second they rested on her. "You may very well have some means of access unavailable to me."

"You mean, like I could talk to the officers involved, undercover-like?" She wondered why they hadn't gone into his office. It couldn't be healthy for the investigation—or her, for that matter—if the two of them were seen talking together too much. Especially if they were going to work together.

He touched her elbow gently and directed her across the corridor. "This room has a video camera," he explained as he opened the door.

"What are we taping?"

"I have a contract we need to go over and you have to sign. It protects both of us."

"I'm sure," she said.

PART TWO
MOVING ON

CHAPTER TEN

ABEL DELAGUERRA SIGHED AS HE STARED OUT THE SECOND-story window of his villa in the west coast Mexican state of Sinaloa. Today the sweeping vistas of the Sierra Madres brought him scant comfort. His health was excellent, his doctors assured him, and would be for a man half his age. He had planted many seeds in his younger, wilder days. His many children, scattered across three countries, were doing well. His sons were growing into fine young men; his daughters becoming as beautiful as their mothers. He was lord and master of all the land between his home and the mountains. Most men would be content with that, but he wasn't like most men.

He had vision.

He had also suffered several expensive losses in recent weeks. No man would be pleased about that.

He pulled his bathrobe shut and knotted the sash. A major reorganization was called for. Whether his recent reversals were a result of bad luck, fate, or the evil machinations of his enemies, this rash of misfortunes was not to be tolerated. Too many people were watching, waiting to fill his position. If he wasn't constantly in motion, moving forward, then they would soon be pouring dirt on his face. That was the way of the world.

Three weeks ago, one of his planes carrying a huge payload had crashed in the mountains. They had recovered the marijuana, but not the cocaine. He suspected guerrillas had stumbled across the shipment; Lord knew there was enough there to finance a revolution. He was doing what he could to track the missing product; someone would talk soon enough. The business could absorb the loss, but Victoria would have to wait for her silver Jaguar with the zebrawood dashboard and steering wheel. He'd tell his wife that for the craftsmen to meet her exacting standards would take time. Spoiled as she was (and for that he blamed himself), she would accept that.

The worst of this month's bad luck was the death of three of his better soldiers. They had died in a hail of gunfire as they made ready to liberate two of his more daring and successful narcotraffickers. The smugglers had been arrested in a surprise raid and were looking at years in an American prison. Delaguerra knew what a tremendous boost of morale such a rescue would generate.

Not only had the mission failed, but he had lost three more good men. Training and selection took time, time that would not come back, precious effort wasted. He sighed as he considered the years he'd worked on these people, placing them in position, gaining the trust of those they would deceive.

The loss of human life was also a tragedy. He wasn't immune to the survivors' suffering. Sometimes he wished he didn't feel the pain of the people he'd taken into his protection. When possible and practical, he made it a point personally to deliver the sad news that the job often generated.

It wouldn't do for him to be bleary-eyed, smelling of bad habits, and unkempt when he made these calls. This set a poor example. Also, to show up drunk would show a terrible lack of respect. He sipped his chili-spiced chocolate, made the Mexican way. His only vice.

Perhaps he should get some exercise in. An article he'd read in one of Victoria's American magazines touted aerobics as an effective means to battle depression. God knew, his shoulders were heavy with the weight of widows' tears and their doe-eyed children. Some days, the burdens of his business outweighed its creature comforts.

"Oh, no," Victoria wailed from the garden below.

Shit, he thought, *what now?* He stepped out to the patio and looked down.

Victoria stood with her hands in her long black hair. The object of her concern was a large trellised rose she had trained to cover the arbor. "You've ruined it."

The gardener stood in the shadow of her wrath, his expression one of overacted innocence. A pair of garden loppers hung from his hand, the tool's sharpened ends just touching the sun-baked earth at their feet.

Abel set down his cup. "Do I have to do everything?" he yelled to no one in particular.

Victoria looked up and saw him. Some women look beautiful when they're mad. His wife's anger had the opposite effect. Her lips pulled back unbecomingly to show more of her gums than he cared to see, the skin around her eyes puckered, and the whites turned red. His stomach soured at the prospect of hearing about her stupid fucking roses for the next week. He slammed the bedroom door after himself as he made for the stairs.

The gardener cowered as Abel approached. This only brought to mind the worker's previous lack of respect, which in turn only fueled Abel's anger. He saw the thick severed rose stalk intertwined with the healthy vines. What a mess. Stupid peasant. He was surrounded by imbeciles. How did one expect to soar with eagles when surrounded by goat fuckers?

Victoria pointed to the base of the plant, where the stem had been severed almost in two. "Send him back to the fields," she said.

As if Abel would keep one so careless on his staff. He pulled his pistol from his pocket and held it to the gardener's head. Victoria shut up.

"You want him back in the fields?" Abel asked.

Victoria didn't seem so sure of herself now.

Abel pressed the barrel to the man's temple. "You want me to take care of this?" The gardener tried to tilt his head away from the gun. Abel grabbed him roughly by the sleeve, holding him upright. A dark stain spread at the crotch of the gardener's pants. Abel didn't need to look at the expression on the man's face now. He knew what it would be.

Victoria raised her hands, palms facing each other as if she were about to clasp them in prayer. "You don't have to do this."

Abel felt his heart rev, speeding the blood through his veins. "Yes? Now you are going to tell me what I need to do?" With a quick movement, he compensated for the gardener's flinch and pulled the trigger. The man crumpled, dead before he hit the ground. "Now you need to get a new gardener. Can you handle that?"

"Yes," Victoria said in a small voice.

"You're sure? I could make all your decisions for you. Is that what you want?"

She shook her head no. Her lips parted slightly but no words emerged.

Abel felt a grim satisfaction. She was much prettier when she was frightened and vulnerable.

At the sound of the shot, Humberto, Abel's second, came running from the house with his gun drawn. Humberto was surprisingly quick for such a big man.

"It's okay now," Abel said.

Humberto holstered his pistol, but his forehead still wrinkled with concern.

Abel knew Humberto was worried that security had been breached, that he had failed at his job. Abel put his mind at ease. "Don't worry; this one was never a threat."

"What do you want me to do?" Humberto asked, his expression still anything but relaxed.

Abel nudged the dead gardener with the toe of his slipper. "You know his name?"

"Nestor," Victoria said, her hand to her throat. She looked as if she was fighting off tears. At least she wasn't yelling anymore. Praise God for small favors.

Abel turned to his lieutenant. "Find out if he has any other family working for me and take care of them."

Humberto nodded and Abel was pleased to see the respect in the other man's eyes. It never hurt to reinforce his position now and then.

He grabbed Victoria's long hair and pulled her head back for a kiss. "Go upstairs. I'll be there in a minute." He slapped her ass, feeling better already.

"And when I find the family?" Humberto asked.

"The usual." Abel dismissed the man with a curt wave, his mind already on the pleasures that awaited him upstairs in his bed. He was glad the children were at school. Their mother could be loud. Humberto would see to the details about the other thing. He was a good soldier and knew what his *patrón* wanted.

No matter what, Abel Delaguerra always took care of the families. It was the only way he slept at night. "And Humberto? Make it quick. I need you to go to Los Angeles."

CHAPTER ELEVEN

MUNCH TOOK A SEAT AT AN INNOCUOUS WOODEN TABLE. Unlike most furniture found in interrogation rooms, there was no graffiti scratched into the top. It was, however, bolted to the floor. The camera was not concealed. Apparently any subjects who found themselves in this room knew full well they were being recorded and there was no need for subterfuge.

Bayless Xeroxed her driver's license and took her fingerprints. "We'll need to call up your criminal record and include it in the file."

"Whatever floats your boat," she said.

He put a contract before her. "I'll need you to initial each page as we go through them."

Munch lifted the hefty document. "This could take some time."

"Some stipulations won't apply."

"That's a relief."

He smiled in that nervous manner of his that she still hadn't figured out. You'd think if anyone's conscience was clear, it would be his. Cops didn't get transferred into IA unless they were squeaky clean.

"Ready?" he asked.

"Sure."

Bayless started the camera and sat down opposite her. "State your name."

"Miranda Mancini." She smiled at the camera, then looked back at him. He also asked her age, her citizenship, and whether she was a public official, employee of a financial institution or school, member of the military service, a representative or affiliate of the media, or a party to or in position to be a party to privileged communications, such as a member of the clergy, a physician, or an attorney.

After she had said no to everything, he smiled apologetically. "As I said, many of these clauses are nonapplicable, but we need to go through the list."

"By all means," she said, smiling to put him at ease, "dot your i's."

"Are you now or have you ever been a substance abuser?"

She looked at him, then at the camera, then back at him. Deciding this would look shifty as hell, she resolved to keep her attention focused solely on Bayless. She didn't know to whom this videotape would be shown, or how much that audience would understand about recovery. "I used drugs years ago. I have been completely clean and sober for nine years."

"Do you have any relatives in law enforcement or under their employ?"

"Not to my knowledge," she said.

He twitched. "Can you clarify this statement, please?"

"I have no living relatives that I know of." She wanted to add that she was a self-made orphan, but didn't think this the time for her to reveal her wit. Not everyone got her. Major understatement.

"Is your decision to aid in this investigation voluntary, and will the information you provide be truthful?"

She hesitated only a second. "Yes."

"The Los Angeles Police Department will strive to protect your identity."

She nodded. At least he wasn't making any promises he might not be able to keep. They paused while she initialed pages.

He cleared his throat. "I have some additional instructions."

She was again seized with the desire to alleviate his angst. Maybe that was his game.

"First," he said, "you must abide by all instructions."

"Okay." She almost smiled. Ask any mechanic; instructions were the things you read when all else failed.

"You are not an employee of the LAPD and you must not represent yourself as such. This means you can't enter any contracts or make any promises on behalf of the department."

"Fine." She wondered what past cluster fuck had made that rule necessary to spell out.

"You can't carry a gun, controlled substances, or engage in any criminal activity."

"I wasn't planning on it."

"The department cannot guarantee any rewards, payments, or other compensations to you in your role as a confidential informant, or CI."

Or snitch, Munch thought. She looked at the camera and said, "That's not what I'm about."

Bayless held up his index finger as he continued to read from his crib sheet. "In the event that the CI receives any awards, payments, or other compensation from the Justice Department, the CI is liable for any taxes that may be owed."

"Oh, that's just beautiful," Munch said.

"I'll need you to sign a confidentiality agreement, also. Please read it carefully."

Munch waded through the legalese. Basically, she agreed in signing this last document that she would not divulge the information she was about to receive under penalty of jail time and/or fines. She wondered if those fines were tax-deductible.

"All right," she said, pushing the last of the papers back to him. "What do you want me to do?"

Bayless turned off the camera and brought his chair around so that the table no longer separated them. "The cocaine business has brought in a lot of money to the city. With money comes temptation."

"I'm sure that's true." Munch tried to keep her posture relaxed and nondefensive. She was here to expose the truth and prove to this guy that Rico wasn't dirty, but she didn't want to appear close-minded.

Bayless picked at an imaginary nit on the knee of his slacks. "Are you familiar with the CCE act and the asset seizure laws?"

"Sort of. What does CCE stand for?"

"Continuing Criminal Enterprises."

"Sounds like a rock band."

Bayless went on as if she hadn't spoken. Not even a smile. "When someone is found in the possession of illegal drugs, no matter how small the amount, his or her money and other property are subject to seizure by the arresting officer."

She always thought that law sucked but wasn't going to offer her opinion unless asked. Hadn't she just signed on to be a team player?

Bayless leaned forward in his chair and folded his hands loosely between his knees. "In theory, forfeiture is meant to punish drug kingpins by taking away their toys. In practice, it is an invitation for terrible abuse of power."

Munch shifted to attention. Maybe her and Bayless's beliefs weren't so far apart after all. "Go on."

"Case agents get their pick of seized cars. I've seen cases where people with no criminal record, but really cool rides, suddenly come under indictment and the next thing you know their car is in our lot."

"And this ties to Rico's case how?" Munch asked, already thinking about the Shelby Mustang.

"The officers who shot him were under investigation for just that."

Munch exhaled. No wonder he didn't want her carrying a gun. "So we nail one of them for that and maybe he'll roll on his buddies for the shooting."

"How good an actress are you?" Bayless asked.

"You'd be amazed."

"Here's the plan: I'm going to plant some information about you not being happy about the reasons you've been given about your fiancé's death."

"And for this I need to act?"

His smile came and left so quickly that she wasn't sure she'd seen his lips move. "You can't let on you know any of the things we've discussed, and especially not that you're helping me."

"I can do that."

"And in the future, don't call me. I'll call you."

"When can I expect that?"

"As soon as it needs to be. Don't worry, I'll be in touch."

Munch got home at noon. Jasper treated her like a long-lost love. She took the time to pet him and tell him how much she loved him, but it felt as if she were just giving him lip service. Petting him didn't give her the pleasure it usually did. She noticed the same sort of thing around Asia. A layer of insulation had grown around her heart, keeping out the good and the bad feelings. She wondered if this was going to be a permanent change.

There were no messages on her answering machine. She opened the refrigerator out of habit. Caroline St. John had dropped off a casserole. Munch decided to save it for dinner. Life went on no matter how you were feeling. You had to act as if something would matter later. She'd been down the fake-it-till-you-make-it road before.

Rico's coat hung in her bedroom closet. She stared at it a minute before reaching into the pocket for his address book. She needed to go through it and call everyone he knew to give them the news and the time of the funeral if they were interested. Not everyone read the obituaries faithfully.

The mortuary had given Fernando a form to fill out for the public notice, and Munch had offered to take care of that for him. Free obituaries were a line or two and listed only the deceased's name and that of the mortuary, along with the phone number of the funeral home.

Those obits had always seemed so sad to Munch, as if no one was left or cared enough to give some sort of accounting of the person's life and passing. The longer obits were paid for. There were also symbols that could be purchased to appear to the left of the name: hearts, flags, roses. She chose a police badge. Like many recent decisions, this was a tough one. She would only have one chance at this and she wanted to do it right.

She started with the statistics of Rico's birthplace and -date, and then added that he was cherished by many and killed way too young. She also listed the loved ones who survived him, as well as those who had preceded him in death. She cried the whole time she wrote it, and was glad for the opportunity. She'd read somewhere that the brain produced endorphin when tears were shed. Some trade-off!

She hesitated a moment before opening Rico's little address book, trying to prepare herself for the surprises it might contain—other women he might have loved or who had loved him. She knew that shouldn't matter now, but knowing and feeling were two different beasts.

Stuck to the black vinyl cover of the address book was a scrap of paper. There was an address written on it in Rico's street writing, not the clear block letters he used when filling out a police report or a shopping list, but a barely legible scrawl. She realized she had been there when he wrote it. It was the information he had recorded from the gang-banger with the pit bull. She flattened the crumpled scrap with her hand and stuck it in the novel by her bed. Then she opened the address book and picked up the phone. Art Becker's home and work numbers were listed. She went with the work number.

Art Becker had been Rico's partner when he worked homicide. She got to know both men when they were investigating the deaths of Ellen's mom and stepdad. Rico she had gotten to know a lot better.

Art Becker had always treated her decently. He was a complex man, capable of gentleness, but certainly not gullible. A detective for twenty years, Becker was on the backside of fifty, and still married to his original wife. The last, she knew, was a real rarity among cops. She wasn't exactly the poster child for monogamy, but she admired it in others. Had she been given the chance, she had planned on being a really good wife.

"I've been meaning to call you," he said, once she had identified herself.

"That would have been nice."

"No, really, I mean it. In fact, let's meet for coffee. How're you holding up?"

"I don't know. I was hoping you could shed some light. There's a lot of bullshit flying."

"Tell me about it. You know that pie place in Santa Monica?"

"The House of Pies?"

"That's the one. Can you be there in twenty?"

She looked at her watch, as if that had anything to do with how fast she drove. "Sure."

"I'll tell you what I know, but it's not much."

"I'd really appreciate that. I've been feeling kind of . . . lost." She cleared her throat, wiped the tears from her eyes as they formed, and got her emotions under control. "How come there hasn't been anything on the news about the shooting?"

"We can talk about that, too."

"Thanks, Art."

"For what?"

"For not disappearing on me."

"Sure, kid. Sure." His voice was gentle. "Drive safely, there's sharks in the water."

"Isn't the expression 'blood in the water'?"

"Right now, there's both."

CHAPTER TWELVE

ART BECKER HAD PICKED THE HOUSE OF PIES FOR MANY reasons, Munch figured. Proximity, privacy, and the chocolate silk with Bavarian cream and semi-sweet shavings. Becker was a formidable man. Under six feet and over three hundred pounds. He barely managed to squeeze in between the booth's high-backed seat and fixed table.

The waitress came and took their orders.

Munch studied Becker's face as she sat across from him.

If the events of the past week had added lines to his face, she couldn't tell. Becker's complexion had always been a study of craters and crevices. His eyes were small, but not cold. At least not to her.

She got right to it. "They told his ex-wife that he was a dirty cop. They're threatening to deny all his benefits."

Becker mopped sweat off his forehead with a napkin. "I know."

"I don't believe it; do you?"

Becker sighed. "I don't want to. I've been a cop for thirty years, most of those working major crimes. I've seen too many things that defy explanation."

She didn't expect any more or less from him. "Have you known any dirty cops?"

"There've been a few."

"How does that happen? Do they sour on life? Get greedy? What?"

"Most of the dirty ones are bad before they ever join. I got a friend who works in personnel, doing background checks on applicants. Ever since this, whatchamacallit, affirmative action shit passed, we've been hard-pressed to meet thc quotas. He showed me three applicants' sheets last month. Two had juvenile beefs, one being a homicide. The third had been indicted, but not convicted, for assault with a deadly weapon. My friend's captain tells him he's gotta pick two of them."

"Harsh." The next question she was almost afraid to ask. "Are you coming to the funeral?"

"Sure. Of course."

She blinked back tears and got busy with her napkin. Rico had been lucky to count Becker as a friend. "When can the family have the body?"

"Hasn't the department sent a liaison over to help with all that?"

"Considering the circumstances, the family has refused to work with the department."

"Probably just as well," Becker said. "I hate the bullshit that goes with cop funerals. All those politico assholes using the day as an excuse to get before a camera. Desk jockeys who've never seen action and wouldn't deign to acknowledge a workingman if it didn't further their career, acting like they give a shit."

"I don't think that would happen with Rico. You know, considering."

"Nothing would surprise me. The department always shows two faces. No matter what the internal gossip is, they wouldn't miss an opportunity to service their own agenda." He looked around impatiently for the waitress, as if his agitation had fueled his appetite. "I'll call the coroner when I get back to the office, make sure he's done on his end. Have you made arrangements with a mortuary?"

"His father wants to use the same home that handled his mother."

"Oh, yeah, Christ, that's right. She passed not that long ago."

"Coming up on a year in June. Poor guy, they'd been married forever."

Becker nodded. "What kind of service are they having?"

"What do you mean?"

"Are they having Rico buried or cremated?"

"Buried."

"That gets pricey, what with the embalming and coffin, and all. You sure they want to go that route?"

"They're Catholic. They don't burn their dead, something about respecting the bodies of the deceased and honoring the places they rest."

"I'm just trying to save you-all some expense. People always spend too much money on funerals."

Munch clenched her fists under the table. "I don't think we'll change our minds. There's gonna be a vigil with all the rites and prayers. Just the family and close friends are invited. They've got the church reserved for Friday. The body is supposed to be present for that so we can say our good-byes."

Becker looked out the window, then back at her. "I don't think you'll want an open casket."

She didn't want to ask, but her mouth formed the words anyway. "Why is that?"

The waitress set Becker's pie in front of him and told Munch she'd be right back. Becker didn't dig in immediately and waited for the server to leave before he continued. "Gunshot wounds get kinda messy, especially multiple ones."

She started scratching at a spot on her thumb and couldn't seem to stop herself. She knew Rico had been shot dead; she hadn't expected further details such as how many bullets had hit him and where to make her feel worse. Becker took her silence and filled it.

"Your mortician is gonna need current photographs to reconstruct his features, but are you sure that's the way you want to remember him? Maybe you could just put a nice framed picture on top of the casket. I've seen them do that."

Munch nodded. "I've seen that, too." He might as well have stuck his fork into her chest. She massaged the ache there, wondering if this was what a heart attack felt like. St. John had once described it to her, said that it felt like an elephant was standing on his chest. Since Monday, she'd been swallowing aspirin like candy, wishing she could use something stronger.

The waitress delivered Munch's order, looked briefly at the expressions on Munch's and Becker's face, and left without asking if they were all right or needed anything else.

Becker carved off a wedge of his dessert and shoveled it into his mouth.

Munch cleared her throat and made an attempt at her apple pie. "Do you know about the case he was working on?"

Becker shook his head before he started talking. "I couldn't talk about it if I did. The indictments are still sealed. The DA wouldn't jeopardize his case for love nor money."

Munch slid the pie around her plate. "I was thinking, maybe it was a case of, like, friendly fire. You know, Rico is working his case and these other narcs from another division are working theirs, and the second group of narcs don't realize Rico is one of theirs. . . ." She stopped talking because Becker was shaking his head again.

"Wouldn't happen. All investigations go through a clearinghouse. They keep a war board that shows all ongoing operations. They got photos of the cops, license plates and makes of the undercover vehicles, times and locations when and where buys are going down. All that to prevent just that sort of thing."

"Oh," she said. "I was just thinking, you know, that might explain it. Everyone makes mistakes."

"It happened in the seventies a couple times, cop versus cop. One buying, one selling, then everyone flashes their badges and not a bad guy in sight."

"I was just thinking of possibilities, like I said."

"I thought you'd want the truth," he said gently.

"Yeah, no, I do." She doctored her coffee, her theory dissolving like the sugar. She'd really pinned her hopes on that explanation. It took her a while to be able to look at him again. She wanted to ask the right questions, but she was drawing blanks. She felt as if she were trying to crack a time-controlled bank vault; one wrong turn and the mechanism would lock up for hours she didn't have. "When will the indictments get unsealed?"

"Hard to say, honey. Hard to say." He scraped the last of the whipped cream from his plate. "Might be some time. Depends on the size and scope of the case."

She pushed her pie away uneaten. "I'll talk to the family, you know, about the body."

"Get multiple copies of the death certificate, at least five. That'll come up a lot." He picked up the check and patted her hand. "I'm sorry it has to be this way."

"Me, too."

It wasn't until she left the restaurant that a new theory presented itself. A wild one, true, but it all made sense. The denial of his benefits, the unwillingness to have his body viewed openly. He was still alive. Rico was still alive. For some reason he had to stay deep undercover and couldn't tell anyone. It was cruel, but plausible. Wasn't it? Asia had seen it first. Little kids had such clarity sometimes.

Munch didn't look at herself in the rearview mirror as she formed these thoughts. She hated it when anyone, including herself, lied to her face.

The whoop of a siren drew her attention. The black-and-white behind her flashed its lights and the cop gestured for her to pull over. She automatically reached down and buckled her seat belt before complying.

She waited while the cop approached. They preferred you stay in the car. She never quite got the logic of that. Seemed to her that she was more dangerous in the car. She could have a weapon on her lap or just whip it in gear and take off once the cop was out of his unit.

"License, please," he said.

"You want my registration, too?"

"Are you the owner of this vehicle?"

"Yes."

"Miranda Mancini?"

"Yes."

He opened her door. "Step outside, please."

"What's this about?"

"Lock up your car. I need you to come with me."

"Am I under arrest?"

"Only if you don't come willingly."

CHAPTER THIRTEEN

THE COP WAITED WHILE MUNCH LOCKED HER CAR. SHE PUT her keys in her purse.

"Anything in your pockets?" the cop asked, taking her bag.

"No." She turned them inside out to prove it.

He opened the back door of his cruiser and she got in. At least he wasn't cuffing her. The trunk opened behind her and then was slammed shut. When the cop returned to the driver's seat, he was no longer carrying her purse.

The patrol car stank of cleaning solvents and some acrid undertone of human origin. The bench seat was ripped and poorly repaired with duct tape. It also rocked as they turned corners, the bolts holding it to its brackets having been dispensed with long ago. Munch had visions of similar rides years ago and of her younger self furtively trying to ditch contraband only to have it discovered when they arrived at the police station.

Munch looked out the window, not recognizing the streets.

"Where are we going?" she asked the cop.

"We're almost there," he said.

Maybe this was a shortcut, she thought. Or maybe it was a one-way trip. A brief, all-purpose prayer came to mind.

Fuck it.

Minutes later, they pulled into the Pacific Station on Culver Boulevard. Rico's station.

The cop drove into the underground parking structure and

parked. The trunk lid opened behind her and she heard men's voices talking in tones too muted for her to decipher the words.

She sat in the patrol car another five minutes, then another cop, this one a woman, escorted her through the double locked doors to the lockup.

"Wait here," the woman said, indicating a wooden bench along the concrete wall.

Munch glanced at the clock mounted high on the wall. It too was caged, but she took some small comfort in being able to keep track of the time. It was one-thirty. Asia's bus would be delivering her to Munch's workplace in two hours. The Texaco station was in Brentwood and Munch's car was in Santa Monica.

She doubted very much if her present business would conclude in time for her to pick up her daughter. Her boss, Lou, would watch Asia until the end of the business day. A better plan would be to have Ellen take Asia home; then Jasper would be covered, too.

Munch was alone except for the woman cop, who was now typing in the cubicle across the room. The nameplate on her desk read FRANCES NEAGLEY. Munch leaned over and saw a hand-painted rock weighing down a stack of reports. A misshapen clay bowl held paper clips. Munch had similar treasures crafted by Asia adorning her home.

"Excuse me."

Officer Neagley stopped pressing keys and looked at Munch.

"I need to check on my kid." Munch pointed to the telephone on the women's desk. "May I use your phone?"

"No." Neagley resumed typing.

Bitch. So much for motherhood solidarity.

Another fifteen minutes passed while Munch watched the clock and jiggled her leg. Frances Neagley crooked a finger at Munch. "Stand by that door. When you hear the buzz, push it open."

"And the magic word is . . . ?"

"Now," the bitch cop said.

Munch flushed with anger and embarrassment. She got sober so she wouldn't have to put up with these power games. If Rico were still here, still alive, none of this would be happening.

The buzzer sounded and she pushed the door open. The cop who had brought her there was waiting for her. He printed her, stood her against the wall and took her picture with a Polaroid camera. She cleaned the ink from her fingers while the picture developed.

The cop showed her the finished product. "You look pissed off," he said.

"Imagine that." She wished he hadn't said "pissed off," because now she realized she had to use the bathroom. Rather than risk another no, she held it.

The cop took her to a room filled with file cabinets, legal storage boxes stacked against the wall, and two desks in opposite corners. In one corner, a large-gutted Latino detective talked to another guy with multiple tattoos. Munch sat in the chair next to the unoccupied desk. She scanned the desktop, looking for clues, but the file folders were all closed. Corners of photographs peeked out from beneath the midden, but nothing more than background showed. The nameplate next to the in-tray read DET. CHAPMAN. She fantasized accidentally knocking it all over with her elbow.

Finally a second detective entered the room and strode across the floor toward her. The suit jacket hanging on the rack behind his desk matched his pants. He dropped a large file on the blotter. It landed with a slap. Munch flinched, though she tried not to.

Chapman sat behind his desk, black-rimmed cheaters perched low on his nose, and perused the file. Periodically he looked at Munch, then back at his reading material.

"Okay," she said, "you win. What's this all about?"

"I win what?" he asked.

"I'll talk, I'll sing, I'll stand on my head. Just give me a break with the silent treatment."

Chapman said absolutely nothing for the next five minutes. Munch timed him.

"Can I use the phone?" she asked.

"Who do you want to call?"

Munch looked at the clock, remembering what St. John had said about narcs, how they'd use anything against her. "I thought I'd order pizza."

Chapman gazed at her over the top of his reading glasses. "A smart-ass, huh?"

"Hey, this is your party."

He threw the file down. "You've had quite the life."

"I'm still having it."

He smiled despite himself. "Why do you think you're here?"

"My fiancé is dead. You think he was dirty and that I might know something about that."

He nodded thoughtfully. If he was surprised that she skipped the dance, he didn't show it. "Do you want to help us?"

"I want everyone to get what they deserve." She watched his face and body language closely, hoping to get a read on this guy. Did he want what he was due or did he fear it? In the immortal words of Jiminy Cricket, *Let your conscience be your guide, motherfucker*. Okay, maybe Disney characters didn't curse, but you could tell they were thinking it.

Chapman's reaction, whatever it was going to be, was cut short by his ringing phone. He answered on the first ring. "Narcotics." He looked at her as he spoke into the phone. "Uh-huh. Thanks. We'll be right there."

She was led to a small room. Acoustical tiles covered the walls as well as the ceiling. There were three chairs and no table, and, as far as she could detect, no camera either. A second cop joined them. He was dressed in jeans, T-shirt, and work boots. His hair was down to his collar and a lighter brown than his Fu Manchu mustache. He wore his badge on a chain around his neck. She realized that they were the two cops she'd seen in Rico's driveway. The ones in the Shelby.

Munch remained standing. "Are you supposed to be Starsky or Hutch?"

He smiled like a Boy Scout. She hoped he didn't grin like that when he was undercover or he was looking at a short and unsuccessful career.

"Munch, isn't it?" He patted the seat of one of the chairs, and perched on the arm of another. "Call me Roger. You've met Detective Chapman, I see."

She sat. "Not formally, Rodge."

Chapman closed the door. The remaining chair had no arms. Detective Chapman dragged it over to the wall opposite the door and sat. Munch's back was to the door, but she didn't mind. She already knew she wasn't going to leave until she reached a working agreement with these guys.

Roger leaned toward her. She mirrored his gesture.

"Let me begin by saying that I know it's been a rough time for you."

"Thanks." She looked around her pointedly. "Every day keeps getting worse."

Roger was all sympathy. "I'm sure."

"I know there are things you can't tell me," she said, "but someday the truth will come out."

Chapman spoke now. "And what will that be?"

"What I've said all along. That Rico was a good man and a good cop."

Chapman loosened his tie. "A lot of people wouldn't agree with you."

"How can we prove them wrong?" Roger asked.

Munch raised a hand. "Let me ask you one question first."

"What's that?" Roger said.

She locked on his face. "Were you the ones who killed him?"

They were temporarily dumbfounded, too surprised to be angry at being asked a question by the subject they were interrogating. When they answered, it was in unison. "No."

Munch wasn't sure what to believe. In her experience, lies came out quicker than the truth, especially rehearsed ones.

"So what's it going to take?" Munch asked.

"How far are you willing to go?" Roger asked.

"I can try to get close to the guys Rico was supposedly in with."

A look passed between the two detectives. It was the mental high five between con men when their plan falls into place quicker than they had anticipated.

Detective Chapman's eyes narrowed first as he remembered his character's role in this production. "Why would you do that?"

"Because everyone else seems pretty content to accept the idea that Rico was crooked. Shit, the city saves itself a bunch of money. How hard are they gonna want to look?"

"This isn't about money," Chapman said.

Munch shot him a *yeah, right* look.

Roger scratched his head. "But what makes you think you'll be able to find out anything?"

"I'll be hanging with the women and children. If the old ladies don't talk, the kids will."

"We'll have to check with our lieutenant and there's some paperwork that will have to be done."

"What kind of paperwork?" Munch hoped she was putting just the right amount of suspicion into her tone.

"A contract," Chapman said, tightening his tie. "If you work with us, it will be in the capacity of a confidential informant. We can do this now, get it out of the way."

"When does Asia get out of school?" Roger asked.

"Three-thirty." Munch knew she shouldn't be surprised. Of course they knew about Asia. For that matter, these cops might have been Rico's friends—as in the who-needs-enemies variety. "If I could make a quick call, I'll arrange for someone to look after her, then I'm all yours."

Chapman gave Munch some change and then walked her over to

the pay phone in the hallway. She called Lou. As soon as her boss answered, she heard a second small click. It came as no surprise to her that the pay phone was bugged. She told Lou she would be late picking up Asia after school. He told her it wasn't a problem and asked if she was okay.

"Yeah," she told him, "I'm just taking care of some unexpected business that came up."

The two narcs took Munch into a larger room. This one was decorated with fake plants, a couch, and framed paintings on the walls. She was moving up, it seemed.

For the second time that day, Munch was walked through the rules governing her status as a CI.

"Are you willing to take a polygraph?" Chapman asked when she had signed and initialed all their documents.

"Waste of time," Munch said.

"Is that a yes or a no?" Chapman pressed.

"Go ahead and hook me up," she said. She didn't have to look in a mirror to know her eyes were dry and flat. She heard it in her voice, too. Her emotions had leveled out to a slow steady burn. She knew how to feed off the energy her anger generated. Fire had been her plaything all her life, it seemed.

They took her to another room where a polygraph examiner had set up his machine. A tube was run around her chest, and other sensors monitored pulse and respiration. She was instructed to limit her answers to yes and no. Munch nodded. She knew the rules.

The examiner asked her if her name was Miranda Mancini.

"Yes," she said.

The examiner noted the movement of his needles across the readout tape. Chapman and Rodger watched over the guy's shoulder.

"Ask me again," Munch said.

"Is your name Miranda Mancini?"

This time she answered, "No."

Munch also didn't have to see to know that the movement of the needles was identical to when she'd given the opposite answer a moment ago. It was all about controlling the burn.

The examiner looked at the detectives, obviously annoyed. "Do you want me to continue?"

Chapman and Roger conferred in whispers. Two minutes later Munch had been unhooked from the machine. They returned to the room with the plants and the cops gave her some last-minute advice.

"When you meet with these guys, be careful not to get caught in a lie," Chapman said. "Speak in vague, knowing terms."

Munch knew this technique by another name, one that involved male bovines and their excrement.

"Act like you know what's going on without being specific," Roger added. "Remember to shut up and let them fill in the silence. Any other questions?"

"Will I get paid?"

"We have a small discretionary fund for mercenaries," Chapman answered.

Roger looked disappointed at the question.

"I wouldn't ask," Munch said, "but the money I make at the gas station is based solely on commission and I've got bills."

"But your motivations for doing this are as a good citizen, right?" Chapman let a touch of sarcasm emphasize his words.

"I can be a good person and get paid. Wouldn't bother me a bit."

"We'll work something out," Roger said. "But first we'll need a good-faith effort from you."

"Like what?"

"Be creative. Surprise us."

CHAPTER FOURTEEN

THE FOLLOWING MORNING, AFTER DROPPING ASIA OFF AT school, Munch drove over to Ellen's condo. It was Thursday. The mortuary was picking up Rico's body today and bringing it back to Santa Monica to prepare it for the viewing. Before leaving the house, she slipped on the ring he'd given her. It felt loose on her finger. One of many things that weren't fitting lately.

Munch hadn't called ahead. She'd been hearing suspicious clicks on her home phone ever since she'd talked to the cops, and didn't want to alert them to her every move. Now she found herself praying that her friend was home. The building had a locked entrance and an intercom system. Munch pushed the button opposite the name E. SUMMERS and heard the beeps and tones of a phone number being dialed.

"Can I come up?" Munch asked.

"Are you alone? I don't quite have my face on yet."

"I'm alone," Munch said. She needed to get used to saying that again.

The buzzer sounded and Munch pushed the security gate open. Door-jà vu.

Ellen's unit was at the end of a long courtyard, giving her an extra minute to prepare for her callers. When she came to the door, Munch was momentarily speechless. She wasn't used to her friend's honest colors. Barefoot and without the big hair, Ellen was only an inch or two taller than Munch.

Ellen opened the door wide. "What are you waiting for, honey, Christmas?"

"Excuse me, miss; have you seen my friend Ellen?"

"Come on in, I'm getting kind of a late start today."

Ellen's hairpieces adorned Styrofoam heads on a shelf in her closet. She had painted facial features on the forms so that they resembled a lineup of jack-o'-lantern hookers. Her bathroom looked like a closeout sale at a cosmetic factory.

"How soon can you be ready?" Munch asked.

"Depends. What did you have in mind?"

"I want to drop in on some people from Rico's other life." She showed Ellen the address she'd found in Rico's pocket.

"Hmm." Ellen stared into her closet. "Blond and brown, I think." She grabbed a long blond wig that practically screamed *I'm a game puta, amigo*. "You want me to do you, too?"

"Nah, I might need the guy to recognize me."

Thirty minutes later they left in Ellen's car. Their destination was in Venice, more specifically the Hispanic section. Munch knew the area well. In the seventies, she and a bunch of like-minded dopers had lived in an apartment building there which they had affectionately referred to as Tortilla Flats.

The neighborhood hadn't changed much. V13's were spray-painted on the block walls, the signature of the predominant Latino street gang. The small market across the street advertised *masa harina*, dried corn husks, and freshly baked *pan dulce*. The store was also running a special on chorizo. Munch used to love chorizo until she read the list of ingredients on the package. She didn't mind the chemicals, but the pig intestines was much more information than she wanted. Funny she should think of that now. That one of the perils of knowledge was delicious things turning unpalatable.

The address they sought was in the three-hundred block of Hampton Drive between Rose and Sunset Avenues. They turned the corner on Rose to find the street jumping with action.

"What's all this about?" Ellen asked.

"I don't know," Munch said, "but that's our address."

People trudged toward the house as if in the throes of some ancient Mayan dirge. They carried pots and platters of food and cases of soft drinks and beer. Black crepe paper hung from the door. Three pickup trucks with jacked-up suspension and Brahma bull horns fastened to the hoods were parked on the street directly in front, wheels half on the curb. The gun racks were empty, though probably not for long. Two of the trucks' license plates were Mexican. The third was Texan.

Ellen parked halfway down the block, careful not to encroach on the neighboring community known as Ghost Town. There the Shoreline Crips ruled, and white people were only popular as targets.

Munch and Ellen walked the remaining distance to the house. When they got to the yard, an ancient station wagon limped into the carport on mismatched tires. The engine expired with a few protesting knocks and the stench of unburned fuel. Munch immediately diagnosed the cause of the pre-ignition as a too-high idle speed. The idle was probably turned up to compensate for other problems, maybe something as simple as a broken piece of vacuum tubing or retarded timing. She was tempted to offer to have a look, but didn't think her help would go over too big in this neighborhood's macho environment.

The woman driving directed kids of varying ages to carry in the bags of paper plates and plastic utensils stacked around them in the backseat. She opened the tailgate and steam rose from the food packed there.

"Need some help with this?" Munch asked.

"Gracias," the woman said.

"De nada," Munch answered as she hefted a steamer full of tamales.

Ellen followed with a white-frosted cake. "You ever crash a wake before?" she asked out of the side of her mouth.

"Nope," Munch whispered back, as she climbed the steps to the front door. "An autopsy once. But this is a first."

"Lead on, *mi hermana*. In for a peso, in for a pound."

Folding tables in the backyard had been spread with cloths. Vases of handpicked flowers sat between three framed photographs of Latino men. Twenty or so votive candles burned quietly in front of the pictures and plaster busts of Jesus Malverde, the patron saint of drug smugglers.

Rico had explained once that Jesus Malverde was a bandit who met his end as the twentieth century began. According to legend, he was something of a Robin Hood. Having the Mexican government put a price on his head had only improved his reputation. Peppy ballads—*corridos*—told of his martyrdom. Soon after his hanging, locals prayed to his bones and miracles had resulted: lost cows were found, fevers passed, and babies were born healthy.

Jesus Malverde's shrine, built on his remains, was in Culiacán, the capital city of the Mexican state of Sinaloa. The saint's first apostles were the poor highland residents, the classes from which the current crop of drug traffickers emerged. Now offerings were made for a safe drug run north, a bountiful marijuana harvest, and not to be shot again.

Munch had asked Rico what the church thought of this narco-saint.

He had shrugged and said, *You have to remember, it's different down there. Sure, the priests hate that a man who robbed and killed is deified. But what can they do? The people are poor and the police and government are corrupt. Who should their heroes be?*

Munch set the food on the counter in the kitchen, then went out to the backyard to get a closer look at the men in the pictures while Ellen helped arrange the food.

She waited her turn behind young tattooed men with shaved heads. They wore their street uniforms: pressed white T-shirts, creased khaki pants, and thick wool Pendleton overshirts with only the top button fastened. The men genuflected and kissed the religious medals hanging from chains around their necks as they passed the memorial.

Two surly pit bulls watched morosely from behind the chicken wire defining their run. A spring pole used to strengthen the dogs' bite-and-shake muscles hung from a cross beam on a sturdy chain. White foamy drool hung from the dogs' open mouths and strands of glossy mucus looped over their snouts. Munch didn't think the fencing surrounding their small pen thick enough to hold the beasts if they really wanted out.

She walked slowly past the pictures. She didn't recognize the two Hispanic men on either end, but the middle picture was all too familiar.

Rico.

It's a trick. It's all a trick, she reminded herself. Simultaneously another voice in her head told her not to kid herself. It was true. Not only was Rico really dead, but these people were mourning him as one of their own.

"Hey, I know you," a man's voice spoke.

She turned. "Do you?"

"Yeah, I seen you with Enrique. You had that pretty dog. The cocker."

"Okay, yeah. I remember you now. You had the pit bull."

He touched his nose. "I'm Chicken."

She pointed to Rico's and the other men's pictures. "What happened?"

"Were you Enrique's *querida?*"

"More than that." She held up her hand to show off her diamond ring. "We were getting married."

Chicken seemed surprised at the news, but recovered quickly. "I'm sorry, *chica*. You should meet this *varón* over here." Out of the corner of his mouth, in a confidential whisper, Chicken added, "He's just in from Mexico."

Munch nodded, as if this meant something to her.

Chicken seemed pleased to have impressed her as he pointed at a solidly built *hombre* standing by a statue of the Virgin. If the Mexican were a biker, they'd call him something like Tiny, just to make a joke of the obvious. Only he didn't have the beer gut and slovenly hygiene of scooter trash. His fancy cowboy boots added another inch to his impressive build.

She let Chicken lead her through the throng of mourners to the human roadblock.

Her escort presented her as if she were some sort of prize. "This is Enrique's woman. They were to be married."

She realized Chicken didn't know what else to call her. "I'm Munch."

"A terrible thing," the big Mexican said. "*Es verdad*. We all feel the loss."

"And you are?"

"Humberto. If there is anything you need, ask."

"Can you turn back the clock?"

"Sadly, no."

Munch appraised the big man. He really did look bereaved, the way he cast his eyes down, let his lower lip protrude, and crossed his hands in front of his crotch as if he were already graveside.

"What were you to Rico?" Her slip of using his real name was conscious. If they knew him as Enrique, they probably knew a lot more about him—maybe more than her.

"He was known to me. He will be missed."

Munch wanted to scream her frustration. "Look, Bert, let's not be coy, *sabes*? I'm trying to make some kind of peace with this all. You offer help, but I don't know you from Adam. Why would you want to help me anyway? You feeling guilty about something, or are you just a really nice guy?"

Mount Humberto blinked in surprise. He obviously wasn't used to being questioned, certainly not so rudely. Chicken's jaw dropped open, then he swiveled his head to look behind him as if he had heard someone call his name. He slid sideways back into the crowd, taking with him a swath of mourners. The dogs whined, sensing the impending blood sport.

Munch felt a nudge at her side. Ellen had come to stand beside her.

"And did you know that your *novio* was a police?" Humberto asked.

Ellen slapped Munch's arm with the back of her hand. "Didn't I always tell you that?"

"I tried to overlook it," Munch said. "When you're in a relationship, you have to take the whole package, not just the parts you like best."

Humberto's eyes narrowed. You could cut the tension with a machete. Munch wished she had one.

Ellen slowly licked white frosting from her finger, diverting Humberto's attention and most likely the flow of blood in his body. "You want some cake, honey?" Ellen held the large kitchen knife for him to see. As usual, she could go either way.

They waited for Humberto to make the next move.

He looked down at Munch's five-foot frame, then at Ellen's grip on the cake knife and he laughed. It wasn't a cruel laugh as in, *Ha-ha, now I'm going to crush your bones into flour for my bread*. He was amused.

"I am clearly outnumbered and at your mercy, señoras."

Munch pushed down Ellen's knife hand. "So what kind of help are you offering? Rico's work cut him off cold, no pension, nada. They offered to pay to bury him, but we turned them down. I don't want a service that's more for them than for us. Know what I mean?"

Humberto nodded yes. There was intelligence in his eyes. Munch guessed that a lot of people underestimated the big man, saw all that muscle and forgot to take into account that there was a brain there too.

"The family would be lucky to get his last paycheck."

"How much do you need?" he asked.

He was getting right to business. She liked that. "I just want his end. That's only fair."

Humberto appraised her, no doubt wondering how much of Rico's business she knew. His expression was easy to read, a mixture of disapproval and mild alarm. Here in the North, women were unpredictable and far more involved in matters outside the home life than was suitable. Most definitely she was a complication he hadn't expected.

Munch planted her feet firmly, crossed her arms over her chest and held her tongue. Her posture and attitude communicated her sentiments. *Deal with it, macho man.*

When she sneaked a look sideways, Ellen was grinning like an idiot. Her friend didn't get the moniker Crazy Ellen for nothing.

"What is the name of the *funeraria* you wish to use?" Humberto said.

"Galvan and Sons. They're on Pico Boulevard."

"The service will be taken care of. I'll see to it personally."

"And the rest?" Munch asked.

"That is not my decision, but I'll see what I can do. As to his 'end,' as you say." Humberto spread his hand and wiggled it, palm down. "This is something we can discuss. There are always opportunities opening up."

"C'mon, big boy," Ellen said, looping her arm through his. "Let's get you something to eat. I bet your girlfriends can't get enough of you."

Munch exhaled, surprised to realize she felt a strange sense of disappointment as Ellen led Humberto away. When she briefly believed she was about to get her ass kicked, part of her had wanted just that. Some cuts and bruises to go along with her pain. That would show them.

Instead, she had gotten what she came for, hadn't she? It would be insane to want things to get messy. Especially since she had dragged Ellen into her nightmare. Not that Ellen seemed to be minding.

No, Munch was on the path now. She would continue to seek the truth until she found a version she could live with. She looked over at the table in time to see a long-haired Hispanic woman pick up Rico's photograph and plant a large kiss on his face. The Chicana was everything Munch wasn't. Rounded curves, large breasts, long black hair, long red fingernails. One of those juicy young *mamasitas* whose figure would erupt as soon as she started having babies, but by then she would have hooked her man.

Someone called out, "Christina!" and the woman turned.

Christina, Munch thought. *Long black hair*. She felt something inside her snap.

Christina, writer of love notes.

Munch hated her, hated her with every fiber of her being. She strode across the small yard with murder in her heart. The sea of people parted grudgingly.

Munch shrugged aside the hands that would stop her. She was close enough to see the small crescent-moon earring in the cartilage of Christina's left ear. Munch gathered a handful of Christina's hair with one hand and punched her full on the mouth with the other. Christina screamed and clawed at Munch's face. They went down on the dirt. Munch soon gained the advantage, sitting on Christina's belly and raining punches on her face. The spaces between Christina's teeth filled with blood, her long hair collected leaves and dirt. They had rolled close to the dogs' pen and the animals were snarling and throwing themselves against the chain-link fence. Their frenzied activity churned up the uncollected dog shit in their too-small run. Men shouted in Spanish.

Ellen stood above them, brandishing the large kitchen knife. There to ensure that the fight stayed fair and that Munch won.

Finally, strong hands reached down and lifted Munch off the bleeding woman beneath her. Munch felt flush and strong and resisted the arms that encircled her. She tried to bite, but couldn't connect with flesh. She kicked backward, hoping to connect, but the man held her too close for her to do much damage. She realized it was Humberto.

"Let me down," she said. "I can't breathe." His arms encircled her chest. Her feet were at least six inches from the ground.

"Relax," he said.

Munch panted, trying to get more air to her lungs. Strands of Christina's long black hair hung from her still-clenched fist. She shook them off.

Other men helped Christina to her feet. Her face was now punctuated by bright red spots where Munch had punched her. She pointed a finger at Munch and Ellen and promised revenge. Munch felt only the heat of her emotions. It was the best she'd felt in days.

"Let me at the bitch," Munch said.

"You're bleeding," Ellen said.

"Nah, it's not me. I'm fine."

"Yeah, right, you are the winner. Let's just get you to the bathroom."

Humberto brought Munch into the house. Ellen led the way to a bathroom, while the other girl was taken out the front door. Ellen looked in the medicine cabinet and found a bottle of peroxide, then put it back when she saw it was hair-bleaching peroxide and not hydrogen peroxide. Munch turned to the mirror and saw the red bloody stripes on her cheek. The bitch must have scratched her.

Ellen moistened some tissue with water and dabbed at the scratches. "What was all that about?"

Munch told her about the lovers' cards she had found in Rico's desk, and the matching earring in Christina's ear.

"They were probably over long ago. Rico only had eyes for you."

Munch told her about the hair in the brush.

"Could have been his daughter's," Ellen said, not sounding completely convinced of this herself.

"Yeah, maybe." Munch's adrenaline was fading, and she felt slightly nauseous. She also felt stupid for not trying to get any information out of Christina before she started wailing on her. So much for her plan of getting in tight with the women and children.

Ellen produced a tube of antibiotic cream and squeezed a dab onto her finger.

Munch tried to push her hand away. "I'm good."

"I don't want you getting any scars."

"I don't care."

"Maybe not now, but do you really want to think of that skank every time you look in the mirror?"

"Let's just get out of here."

They headed for the front door. Several people patted Munch on the back. Chicken winked at her. Three men and two women were seated on the futon couch in the front room and bent over the spool table before them. The objects of their attention were the rows of glittering cocaine cut on the mirror at their knees. One of the women handed Munch a straw. For a second, Munch almost took it. She saw the hand of a Higher Power here, pairing these two events.

First she lost control and started a fistfight, then barely down from that, she was being offered an engraved invitation to jump back into the life with both feet. She hadn't so much as seen a line of coke in nine years of sobriety. Shit, even when she was using, she had only been offered it for free a few times.

The twelve steps and *The Big Book* of Alcoholics Anonymous made many references to "powers greater than ourselves." It wasn't always specified whether these powers were good or evil. Potent, to be sure.

Munch couldn't pull her eyes away from the free drugs. With all that had happened, who could blame her? Maybe she was being offered a well-deserved break from reality from a loving God who understood her needs.

The scariest part of that thought was how much sense it seemed to make.

"No, thank you," she said, and somehow her feet carried her out the door.

CHAPTER FIFTEEN

DELAGUERRA WATCHED VICTORIA FROM THE DOORWAY OF her studio. She sniffled and touched the edge of her apron to her eyes as she gripped her dry paintbrush and sighed. He wondered what petty bullshit had her down. When he first met her, her hands were stained yellow from stripping the stiff leaves from her family's few acres of coca bushes. She didn't speak a word of English. At thirteen, her back was already assuming the bend of a grandmother. He had saved her from all that and worse. How quickly they forgot.

She could still be in some jungle factory in Colombia, breathing the fumes from the sulfuric acid and petrol used to make the paste that would then be refined into the oily white powder that was his livelihood. Instead, she was living in a beautiful villa, with a driver at her disposal, and anything she desired at her fingertips. Her children attended the finest private schools, where they mingled with the sons and daughters of diplomats, movie stars, and other successful businessmen. She had subscriptions to four different American fashion magazines, which she devoured as soon as they arrived.

All that and she still always seemed to find some reason to be annoyed with him. And one thing about Victoria—she was a genius at letting him know with a million different subtle looks and gestures that he had not lived up to her expectations. And here he was, trying in every manner he could dream of to be a modern man. Sometimes she could be so stupid. A little appreciation for his efforts would go a long way.

Unlike the North, here in Mexico a man was rarely charged and almost never convicted of murdering his wife. Abel didn't believe in violence against women unless it was absolutely necessary. He also conceded that it wouldn't hurt if the Catholic Church modernized some of its views on divorce. He wasn't against dogma. It worked for the masses, but even the local priest agreed that a man in his position could not be and should not be herded with the same staff.

He loved his wife. It wasn't her fault that he had spoiled her. She had given him legitimate children and companionship, and in the early years had been quick to draw a laugh from him. He glanced around her well-lit studio, approving of her use of vibrant colors and bold style. He intended to tell her that today. He knew the compliment would please her, perhaps set an example of behavior that would serve her better. Honey instead of vinegar was what she should be using.

They had come a long way together, and the journey wasn't over yet.

Since the incident with the gardener, she had shown him more respect. At least she hadn't been so quick to snap. God, that it always had to come to some demonstration. This was annoying, but perhaps only human nature. He had skimmed through the books she casually left on his bed stand. Books with titles like *Communication Is Marriage's Strongest Tool* and *Resolving Marital Conflicts: A Psychodynamic Perspective*. Books definitely written by gringos who went to fancy gringo colleges in the North. He would send his sons to those universities when they came of age. Maybe even his daughters as well. Why not?

He paused a moment longer, enjoying the sun on his face, the quiet of his wife's sanctuary. It was almost as if she had managed in this turbulent world of theirs to create an extension of her womb.

In many ways besides the obvious, he preferred women. Even those he used in his business were cooler with their emotions and quicker on their feet than many of his men. His men, his women, hah. So many were looking to move up, hoping to be the next big man. Who was truly loyal anymore? At least one was not. That's all that was certain. Someone had tipped the police about the planned jailbreak. He felt his face harden with sudden fury. When he found out who the traitor was, he would show no mercy.

"Hijo de la puta."

Victoria looked up at the sound of his cursing. She must have been unaware that he was there. Her elbow tipped over her water glass and spilled over the landscape she'd been working on.

"Oh, Abel. Now it is ruined."

He threw his hands up in the air and left the room. Some days a man couldn't win.

"Where to now, slugger?" Ellen asked as they left the wake.

"Rico's," Munch said, feeling suddenly exhausted, even queasy. "The rosary is tomorrow night. I told Fernando I would drop off clothes at the funeral home." She hadn't told him about the photograph for facial reconstruction.

Ellen pulled an illegal U-turn. "You gonna tell the cops you're going over there?"

Munch had considered it. Briefly. "Fuck 'em. What courtesy do I owe any of those motherfuckers?"

"That's the spirit," Ellen said.

Munch felt a little warning chill. First the coke, now this. She knew she needed always to check herself when she gained Ellen's approval.

"I'm just saying I have legitimate reasons."

Ellen made an adjustment to her wig. "Damn straight you do." Ellen's tone was righteous and self-assured, as if she were all about legitimacy and would brook no substitutes.

Munch turned on the radio and let the rock 'n' roll remind her of happier, carefree times. The Grateful Dead started singing about riding that train. She knew all the words. "Casey Jones, you better watch your speed."

They drove along Ocean Boulevard. Past the pier, the four-lane roadway paralleled the strip of park that ran along the top of the cliffs. Benches faced the ocean. A bike trail snaked between wind-gnarled trees and beds of perennials. Joggers and bicyclers avoided the legs of sleeping drunks. Signs warned pet owners that dogs were not allowed.

Santa Monica had a reputation for accommodating the homeless. Cops were instructed to overlook cardboard campsites. Earnest locals passed out hot soup and sandwiches. Clothing and blankets were collected and distributed. Munch was not without compassion, but she believed in carrying the message, not the addict.

Yep, Munch thought, as they turned down into the canyon. The world was seriously mixed up. What other town's library had a sign in the bathroom asking patrons kindly to leave the deodorant dispensers in the toilet bowls?

No dogs, but please bring us your bums.

Ellen parked in Rico's driveway and followed Munch into the house.

Munch went directly to the closet and reached for the uniform in the dry-cleaning bag. The tag on the hanger indicated that the suit had been picked up three weeks ago.

Munch fingered the thin plastic and wondered how it would feel to die with it tied around her face. She shook that image and showed the receipt to Ellen. "It was almost as if he knew that he'd be needing a clean dress uniform."

"My mama had just put up a case of her jam when she was killed. Weird, huh?"

"Yeah, I guess there's always something like that."

Munch got a bag from the kitchen and packed it with a clean set of underwear, shoes, and hat to go with the uniform. She then moved some luggage and lifted the carpet from the floor of the closet to reveal his floor safe.

"You know the combination?" Ellen asked.

"As a matter of fact"—Munch twisted the dial the appropriate turns left and right, then pulled the door open—"I do." She carefully removed Rico's badge and gun, but left the deed to the house and his car. Ellen tossed her a hand towel from the bathroom without having to be asked. Munch resealed the safe and wiped it clean of prints before replacing the carpet and suitcases.

"Where did he keep his wrapping paper?" Ellen asked.

"In the hall closet. There's tape and scissors by the phone in the kitchen."

Ellen held out her hand and Munch handed over the badge and gun. They had hit on this strategy for moving contraband years ago. It took a pretty hard-hearted cop to unwrap a gift he found in the trunk on a routine search. Especially now, when they dressed relatively straight and weren't under the influences of chemicals.

While Ellen got busy in the kitchen, Munch went into Rico's office. She soon discovered that the desk had been completely cleaned out. Even the blotter was gone, along with the love notes and airplane tickets.

Ellen appeared at the doorway carrying a phone-book-sized box wrapped in green shiny paper and tied with a yellow ribbon. "Problem?"

"Somebody took all his papers."

"Those cops?"

"I guess. It doesn't matter. I've got what I need."

Ellen gestured toward the door. "Let's get out of here. This place is starting to give me the creeps."

"It's just a house." Munch reset the alarm before they left. "Brick and mortar. Sticks and stones."

Humberto chuckled as he left the wake. He liked women with fire. Rico must have been some cocksman to invoke such passion. To leave a string of broken hearts in two countries was a legacy to be proud of. Humberto didn't have to wonder who would cry for him when his day came. There was no one. Yet, anyway. He had never attempted to make a woman love him. Now he wondered, How difficult could it be?

Ellen had given him her phone number before the fight broke out. His business in Los Angeles might take as long as a week to conclude, and her company would be much appreciated. And, who knew? Perhaps a little business to mix with pleasure. Part of his agenda of this trip was to put his own distribution agents in place.

He had rented a Chevrolet Monte Carlo. His pickup truck with the Brahma bull horns attached to the hood was a bit too conspicuous, even for Los Angeles. The Chevy was this year's model and vastly disappointing. The vehicle was blue and had a top speed of eighty-five miles per hour, according to the speedometer. Having tested the car engine's horsepower on several of the city's freeways, he was inclined to think eighty-five was an optimistic number. He suspected that the only way the gutless wonder achieved maximum velocity was when it was heading downhill or off a cliff. He might yet put one of those theories to the test. If only to make a statement. A low profile was one thing, but this was ridiculous.

He was on his way to see his cousin. Felix was the son of his mother's brother. The only son and born out of wedlock, therefore somewhat under the radar. Felix worked in the garment district of downtown Los Angeles, selling slightly flawed seconds to the bargain shoppers.

The building where Felix worked was on Hope and Eighth. Humberto parked in one of the all-day lots, happy to leave behind the disappointing American car. Felix's store was on the sixth floor. The large sign over the door read SPORTS APPAREL. Humberto thumbed through the zippered pants and logo-emblazoned sweatshirts looking for any that would accommodate his girth. Felix had yet to notice him. He was busy helping a sharp-faced white woman collect flimsy-looking nylon suits of pants and jackets in a range of sizes.

Felix was small and dark-skinned, but his English was very good, a remarkable accomplishment considering that he had crossed to the North only two years ago. Humberto was proud of him, and sorry that the news he had come to deliver would cause so much grief.

Felix took the woman's money, counted out change, and thanked her for her business. When he had slammed his cash register shut, he noticed Humberto lurking near the doorway.

"Hey, *bueno,*" he said, his face lighting with recognition. "*¿Qué tal?*"

Humberto pulled his cousin to him in a warm embrace. "You're looking good, little brother," he said in Spanish. "The world is treating you well."

"I can't complain," Felix said modestly. "What brings you here?"

"A little of this, a little of that."

"I understand." Felix licked his lips. "How long will you be in town?"

Humberto hesitated before answering. "I'm not sure yet."

"Where are you staying, *carnal?*"

"A motel. It's convenient and near the freeway."

"Nonsense. Stay with me. I have plenty of space, if you don't mind the couch."

"I'm good," Humberto said. "When do you get through here?"

"Five."

"I'll check out some of the other stores and be back before you close. We'll have dinner." His news could wait until then. A few hours would make no difference.

"Is everything all right?" Felix asked.

Humberto rested a big hand on his cousin's thin shoulder. "As well as can be expected. We'll talk more later when we have our privacy."

Felix watched his cousin leave, more than a little concerned. He wondered if they still referred to Humberto back home as the Angel of Death.

Ellen dropped Munch off at her car. "You want to come in?"

Munch seemed to need a moment to think about it. This was uncharacteristic. She was usually so decisive, so clear on her objectives. She never shopped, she bought. "No, I need to go, take care of all this."

"How about later?"

"I guess I'll be home." Munch put the gift-wrapped "present" in her trunk.

Ellen noted the stoop of her friend's back and how her feet seemed to drag. "You want some company?"

"Thanks, but no. I'll be fine. I just need to crash for a while. I haven't been sleeping so good lately."

Ellen gave her a hug, wishing she could magically transfer some life force. "Drive carefully. I'm here if you need me."

Munch nodded her head in seemingly weary acceptance of this fact. "Thanks."

Ellen watched Munch drive off, then let herself into the courtyard of her condo complex, Who would have thought that someday she would be living in a ritzy place like the Oakwood Garden Apartments?

The phone started to ring as Ellen turned her key in the door. It was that big fella, Humberto.

"Miss me already?" she asked.

"I wanted to make sure you made it home all right. How is your friend? The little one?"

"As well as can be expected, I suppose. I've known her for just about ever and I've never seen her so out of her head."

"Will she hurt herself?"

"Now what would make you ask a question like that?"

"I've seen the look before," Humberto said.

"That little gal is pretty tough. You'd be surprised." Ellen thought about the wild light she had seen in Munch's eyes. The girl was crazy with grief. Humberto wasn't wrong about that. Munch and Ellen had pulled some shit together in the past, but since Munch had sobered up, hers had been the voice of reason. Now, Ellen supposed, it was her turn to take the rudder. "If she could just understand what happened. You know, the wondering is the worst part."

"In my country, we have a different saying," Humberto said. "*No se pase de listo*. Maybe I could come over later and explain it."

"That would be right nice." She gave him her address and then checked her party supplies. She liked to think she was ready for anything. Big guys like Humberto tended to let their guards down around the ladies. She'd spent enough of her life in southern California to have a passable comprehension of the Spanish language, with particular emphasis on the dope-related slang. *No se pase de listo* translated to "Don't be too clever." In other words, don't ask too many questions about dangerous subjects.

CHAPTER SIXTEEN

MUNCH TURNED ON HER AIR-CONDITIONING TO ITS COLDest setting and set the blower on high. The scratches on her face were drying, starting to scab. She moved her rearview mirror to study them and noticed that a blue Shelby Mustang was keeping a careful distance of two car lengths behind her. The car had a California license plate. The driver's hands were at the two and ten o'clock position on the steering wheel. She changed lanes without signaling. He did the same. She slowed so she would miss the light, leaving the guy no option but to catch up with her.

She almost laughed out loud when she saw the look of consternation on the driver's mustached face before he pulled his cap down in a half-assed attempt at a disguise. It was her buddy, Roger the not-so-artful dodger.

Munch raised her hand and let it drop, all the while shaking her head at his blatant ineptness. After a second of pretending he hadn't seen her, he waved back. When the light changed, she pulled into the parking lot of a 7-Eleven. Roger pulled up next to her. They both left their engines running.

Rico's uniform was draped over her passenger seat. His hat sat atop his shoes. She had his photograph in her purse.

"What are you up to?" Roger asked in that too-cheery voice.

She pointed to the clothes on her seat. "I'm on the way to the mortuary. You want the address or are you just going to keep following me inconspicuously?"

"So the funeral is Saturday?"

"One o'clock. Why? Are you coming?"

"I'll probably be lurking in the back somewhere. I think it would be better if you didn't acknowledge me."

Suddenly cold, she crossed her arms over her chest, tucking her hands next to her sides. "Were you a friend of Rico's?"

"We knew each other from the job, enough to say hi and shoot the shit."

Now the trembling had reached her legs and she rocked from foot to foot to hide it. "Are you . . ." She ran out of breath before she finished her question and had to fill her lungs and begin again. "Are you sorry he's dead?"

"Of course."

"Will Detective Chapman be there too?"

"Probably, why?"

"I just want to know what to expect," she said. *How many bullets to pack* was what she was really thinking, but she didn't know if Roger-baby would get her humor or if she was even joking. "I don't want a bunch of assholes there that didn't know Rico or who aren't sorry he's dead. I think his family deserves better than that."

"You probably do," Roger said. "But there are bigger forces at work here. The mayor and the chief might not show up, but we'll at least have the assistant chief and his lieutenant. They'll say some words, get their names in the papers, suit up in those uniforms they never wear. Maybe a spot on the evening news if it's a slow news day."

"I was warned about the hypocrisy," Munch said.

"Yeah, well, it's all politics. What happened to your face?"

"I cut myself shaving."

Roger pulled some Polaroids from his coat pocket and handed them to her. "Do either of these guys look familiar?"

Munch felt Roger watch her as she perused the photos. If he was waiting for a reaction, he sorely underestimated her. The two men in the photographs were Hispanic, tattooed, in their twenties, defiant-looking, and very dead. The last she knew because she had just come from their memorial. The captions at the bottom of the photos were dated February 1986. Last month.

"Bad guys?" she asked.

"You recognize them?" Roger sounded impatient now, and there was a touch of challenge to his voice.

Munch didn't know if she had been spotted going in or coming out of the house in Venice, but she had to assume she had. She briefly described the house in Venice and the gangster-style memorial service she had walked into. She left out the part about the fistfight and the cocaine. "I think they were the two guys killed with Rico."

"You're right about that," he said.

"So who were they?"

"Xavier and Candolario Santiago. Brothers and drug traffickers. How did you know about the house on Hampton Drive?"

"I've been contacting Rico's friends to tell them about the services. I found the address in one of his pockets. I'd never been there before, but it could have been someone important to him. I didn't know."

"Did you invite anyone you met there to the service?"

"No, I saw they knew he was dead. There's a notice that will run in the paper tomorrow if anyone is interested." She touched the scratches on her face and recoiled as surprise hit her. "The obit doesn't run until tomorrow, but they knew he was a cop already."

Something switched in Roger's eyes. His face didn't change expression as much as lose all vestiges of one. "Can you go back to the house on Hampton?" he asked.

"Why would I want to?"

"Is that a yes?"

"Yeah, I could go back there. What the hell. They didn't kill me the first time. Humberto said something about me earning some money. I guess I could find out what that's all about."

"You'd be wearing a wire," he said.

"Is that supposed to be comforting?"

"We'll be close by."

"Let's not bullshit each other, okay? If and when I go in there, I'll be alone. If I get made or someone wants me dead, a whole army parked across the street ain't gonna save me."

"Okay, you're right. But you can't work for us and not be monitored. We need to make our case against these guys, and your hearsay ain't gonna get it."

Munch wondered if her past would always shadow her. If know-it-all assholes like Roger would continue to judge her based on a dated rap sheet. People changed. She knew that for certain. Then again, sometimes people changed back. She knew that, too. "When do you want to do this thing?"

"Soon. If it's all right, I'd like to meet you back at your house and show you how the equipment works."

"I've worn a wire before, about six months ago."

"This time will be different."

That's what they all said. "Okay." She looked at her watch. "But it will have to be later, like around five."

"Will Asia be home?"

Munch winced. She hated to hear him call her daughter by name, as if they knew each other, as if they were friends. "Come to think of it, she will. Can we do it tomorrow instead, in the morning, after she's out of the house? Say about nine?"

He changed back into Jolly Roger. "Okay, nine it is."

Munch climbed back in her car. Roger waited for her to take off first. She noticed she had buckled her seat belt and signaled her turn. She usually only drove like that when there was a black-and-white in her rearview mirror.

The funeral home of Galvan & Sons looked like a church. The walls were constructed of antique bricks in alternating hues of terra cotta.

A large evergreen pear tree in full bloom had left a pretty mess of white blossoms on the front lawn and cast the river rock wishing well in perpetual shadow.

A woman in a gray dress greeted Munch as she entered, taking Rico's uniform from her as she asked, "Enrique Chacón?"

"Yes," Munch managed to mutter before a sudden keen escaped her throat. It was a single, high-pitched mewl, a weird and embarrassing sound as if someone had stepped on a mouse. If she loosened her jaw, she might manage a proper howl, but that would be even worse.

The woman patted her shoulder. "Have a seat. Mr. Galvan will be right with you."

The waiting room was filled with comfy sofas, tissue boxes on every table, and discreetly placed hardbound, three-ringed catalogs of caskets and urns. There were also business-card holders with contact information for florists, and some scattered brochures for caterers and limo businesses.

Munch had a small sideline livery service. A&M Limousines. Actually, it was limousine, singular, but most clients booked one car at a time and she networked with a few other single-car operators. So who needed to know?

She was flipping through the photographs of the caskets when the funeral director entered the room.

"Ms. Mancini?"

She lifted her head in a tight-lipped nod to acknowledge him, not trusting herself to speak.

"May I join you?" he asked.

He had a black leather-bound folder which he placed on his lap. The right half of the binder had an invoice clipped to it with "Chacón" written across the top, the other pocket was full of documents.

"Would you like some coffee or water before we begin?" He offered her the box of Kleenex as if they were mints.

Munch grabbed some tissues. "I'll be fine."

Galvan put the box on the table in front of them.

She wrung the tissues in her hands. "Did the, uh, body get here?"

"It arrived this morning."

Munch pulled the photograph from her purse and handed it to him. Rico was smiling one of his awful posed smiles where he thought the object was to show as many teeth as possible. "He was much better-looking than that," she said.

Galvan grabbed the photo by the upper right corner and Munch had to will herself to let go. "We'll do the best we can."

"I brought his hat, too."

"Would you like it resting on his folded hands or on top of the casket?"

"Hands. No . . . casket. No . . . sorry, his hands. Put it on his hands and bury him with it."

Galvan smiled gently. Munch felt the tears rolling down the sides of her face and blotted them with the tissue.

Galvan clicked his pen open and indicated the casket catalog. "We have some floor models downstairs. It might be easier to choose if you can see the actual product."

Munch followed the funeral director downstairs. She was glad for the railing as she concentrated on putting one foot in front of the other. The showroom was brightly lit. Floral arrangements flanked the various caskets lining the walls. The more the coffins cost, she noted, the more impressive the flowers. Caskets were stacked three-high in individual nooks like so many cocoons. The ones on the floor were open, showing off the tufted silk and satin linings. Parked at the base of the room's central support pillar was a stuffed armchair. She wondered who would want to linger here. Maybe it was for the comfort of the bereaved who became too overwhelmed to stand.

Fernando had left the choosing to her. He'd buried his wife in a mahogany box that set him back twenty-five hundred, soup to nuts. She felt herself drawn to the buffed bronze, adding that to the cost of the concrete inner lining to prevent seepage, embalmment, the service, interment, marker, and plot—and the bronze job would bring the total to four large and change.

She told herself that the money spent on the funeral was not the indicator of their love for him. Still, she had earmarked money for the wedding and honeymoon, so it wasn't like she didn't have it. Plus, that Humberto guy said he'd chip in some bucks. She hoped that would happen before he got his big ass busted and his assets seized.

"The bronze."

"And the interior fabric?"

"White satin."

"Very nice."

Munch smiled grimly. At least someone approved of her today. "We're going to need five copies of the death certificate."

Galvan made a note. "No problem."

"Can I see him?"

Galvan's pen stopped moving. "Now?"

"Yeah, I need to. This has all been so unreal."

"It's a little soon. We'll have him cleaned up tomorrow for the viewing." Galvan looked over his shoulder as if seeking help from someone.

Munch put a hand on his sleeve. "It's all right. Just one minute and I'll leave."

Galvan appraised her for a moment. "Wait here, and I'll see if he's presentable."

"Thanks."

Galvan returned a moment later and asked her to follow him. They walked down a hallway devoid of pictures. The floor was concrete, and though there was no draft, the temperature had dropped ten degrees. Galvan pushed through a wide knobless swinging door. He reached back a hand to her as one might to a child when crossing a busy street.

"I'm okay," she tried to say, but she didn't have the wind to push the syllables through her voice box. She filled her lungs, taking with that air the oddly sweet odor of formaldehyde. An embalming pump gleamed in the corner. Glass canisters with stainless steel tops held cotton balls, disposable razors and gauze pads. Scissors, hairbrushes and black plastic combs were spread across the top tray of a wheeled cart.

Rico was laid out on a metal gurney. A sheet covered his body. His skin had almost a greenish tint and his eyelids were flat as if he'd been deflated. The hair above his right ear had been shaved close to reveal an irregular hole. The edges of the jagged wound were charred black. Black bruising extended to his jaw.

Galvan lightly touched the top of Rico's head. "We'll have him looking more natural in time for the viewing."

"Cut the hair and trim the mustache. That wasn't him. He was working undercover."

Galvan looked at her knowingly, as if he had heard it all before. "One ear is pierced. Would you like it to remain empty?"

"What happened to his stud? He had a gold crescent moon."

Galvan checked his paperwork. "There's no mention of it in the property report."

When she had seen the one that bitch Christina was wearing at the house on Hampton, she had assumed it was the other half of the pair. What if it were the same one he had worn? Had he given it to her or had she taken it?

Munch took a deep breath, and to Galvan's dismay, pulled back the sheet covering Rico's body. She gasped at the sight of the autopsy incision, sewn casually shut with widely spaced black stitches.

Galvan gripped her elbow and attempted to pull her away.

"I was hoping . . ." But she never finished her sentence. Her eyes focused unblinking on the torso wounds. There were six, maybe seven holes the diameters of dimes. Cleaned of soot and blood, but looking very unnatural on Rico's familiar chest. For an instant, she had the weird thought that he had grown multiple nipples. Red navels was more like it, innies. Someone had circled the wounds with black ink and numbered them. The numbers began with two. The head shot must have been the first cataloged. He'd received the wound at a close enough range to cause muzzle burn.

Oh, Rico, she thought, *what have they done to you?*

Something also seemed to be written on Rico's shoulder. No, not written. Tattooed. A five-color rainbow with Munch's name written across the top in stylized letters. The symbolism was clear: "Somewhere over the rainbow." It was one of the songs from *The Wizard of Oz,* the same movie that had given Munch her nickname.

She pulled the sheet back up, tucked it in around him, and stroked the cheek that wasn't bruised.

"Treat him good," she told Galvan.

"Of course."

Galvan took her elbow again and she allowed herself to be guided into his office.

"Can I get you anything?" he asked. "You can sit in here as long as you need to, or I can call someone for you."

"I'll be okay," she said, trying to reassure him that this was true. "Thank you. You've been very nice."

Munch left the funeral home surprised to see the world still going on as usual. She had time and then some to get home, pick up the mail, and check her answering machine before Asia's school let out.

St. John had called. He was worried about her and wanted to know how she was. Ditto with her sponsor, Ruby, and Lou from the gas station. Jasper came and sat at her feet with his head on her knee. She stroked his head as she returned St. John's call.

"How are you?" St. John asked. But unlike other people, he waited for the answer.

"I just came from the funeral home," Munch said. She felt deflated and in need of a long sleep. "He's really dead." She described what she had seen in vivid detail.

"What can I do?" St. John asked.

"The funeral mass is tomorrow. I was hoping—" Munch didn't finish her sentence. A loud, unmistakable roar filled the air. Jasper barked at the door, begging to get outside and protect his house.

"Munch?"

"Hang on a second." Munch dragged the phone cord after her to the window and looked out. A dozen Harleys were heading down the street. She locked the dead bolt on her front door. The windows rattled from the vibrations of unmuffled tailpipes. Jasper kept barking at the door, stubby tail wagging in excitement. She looked out the window again and saw that the bikes were backing up to the curb across the street. They gleamed in the midday sun, like so many chrome dominoes. She spoke into the phone, "A bunch of bikers just pulled up across the street."

"Anyone you know?" he asked.

"Uh-oh," she said.

"What?"

"A couple of them are wearing patches."

"What club?" St. John asked.

She squinted. "Satan's Pride. Shit, this is all I need." She told him about the supposed bounty on her head, but not the part about how Rico had promised to put an end to it. She wasn't sure if St. John would approve of blackmailing bad guys, and she didn't want to give anyone more ammo to slander Rico's reputation. Not even St. John.

"You want me to send some black-and-whites over there?" he asked.

"They're leaving now. My neighbor is with them. Nobody's looking this way. I think I'm okay for the moment." She thought about Rico's gun, hidden on the top shelf of her closet. She was going to need it a lot closer than that if it was going to do her any good. "I'm about to pick up Asia from school. Is it all right if she stays with you tonight?"

"Sure, both of you are welcome."

"I'll be okay. I just don't want to be worrying about the kid. I'll bring her dress clothes for tomorrow. You were planning on coming to the mass, weren't you?"

"Of course," he said.

"Thanks. I'll drop her off in a few hours."

"I won't be home, but Caroline will."

"Okay." She was a little relieved not to be seeing him. He might have more questions, and he wouldn't like her answers.

Munch called Bayless next.

He answered his phone like most cops, giving only his rank and last name. He sounded bored and a little annoyed.

"It's Munch Mancini," she said. "I've just come from the funeral home."

"I'm glad you called. I have some good news for you."

She wondered how that was possible.

Bayless cleared his throat. "The department has made a ruling. They're going to bury Detective Chacón with full public honors. I think it's also possible we can reach a settlement so that his survivors receive a stipend."

"Not good enough," she said. She heard the mail truck coming up the block. The mailman liked to rev his engine between stops. The truck also had a bad muffler and squeaky brakes, so every five seconds she and the neighbors were treated to a four-cylinder roar followed by a screech. People who didn't want their ears bent for five minutes also knew to hide when he approached. Munch had learned this the hard way one Saturday. He had waved her mail just out of her reach for ten long minutes discussing world affairs until she finally had to tell him she had left a hose running and a burner on and that she thought she heard her kid crying.

"Don't fight this," Bayless said. "You can't win and it's a good offer. The money will be something to help his daughter through college. You don't want to piss these people off. They'll take the offer off the table and then where will you be?"

About where she was now, she imagined. "In your investigation, did you come across a woman named Christina?" Munch reached down and scratched Jasper's ears. "I don't have a last name. She's Latino, might have some gang affiliations, in her twenties, kind of slutty? Probably sporting a fat lip."

"What about her?"

Munch realized he hadn't confirmed or denied. "Do you know who she is?"

"Listen, take my advice here. Keep your memories. The poor guy isn't around to explain, so just give him the benefit of the doubt."

"That's not going to get it. I know she knew him, maybe even loved him. I also know Rico didn't love her back. I was at the mortuary and I saw Rico's body. He had a new tattoo with my name on it. Why would he get my name tattooed on his arm if he was seeing another woman? What if this bitch was an informant? Maybe she had feelings for Rico that he didn't return, and she set him up."

"Maybe that's so. Not everything adds up. I said that before. Take the deal. And do us both a favor: Forget we ever talked."

"What about the narcs you're investigating?"

"It's handled. Don't worry about them."

"But I have an in, thanks to you."

"I don't know what you're talking about," he said.

She stared at the phone in amazement. What could have possibly happened in the short time since they arranged to work together that would cause this reversal? Who had gotten to him and why? "I can't walk away."

"But that's exactly what you have to do," Bayless said. "You have to walk far away. I'm telling you as much as I can. The officers under investigation have been cleared. You're going to have to trust me. I know you don't know me and you feel jerked around. When I can,

I'll tell you more. Keep your head down, go through your grief process, and try to remember you still have a future. You've worked too hard to get where you are. Don't throw all that away."

"Nobody's throwing anything away." She hung up thinking he didn't understand. She had to prove their whole life hadn't been a lie.

The mailman was turning the corner at the end of the block. Munch hung up the phone and turned to Jasper.

"You want to go for a ride?"

She didn't have to ask twice.

They went out the front door. She opened the car for Jasper and grabbed her mail. There were bills, the usual junk, and a condolence note from the florist who was going to supply her wedding flowers. He probably still wanted her business. Then she came to a cardboard mailer with her name and address written in familiar block letters. The postmark was dated a week ago. There was no return address, but she knew who it was from.

She ripped open the thick envelope and found several Xeroxed documents. The first was a copy of a Confidential Informant application. The document was dated five years earlier, in June of 1981, and the CI was Pete "Petey" Donner, code name "Desert Fox." The other document was a murder indictment dated July of 1981 against members of the Mongols Motorcycle Club, most specifically against the club's president, Albert "Red Al" Cunningham. The district attorney's office named their source and star witness only by his number and code name, "Desert Fox." Munch looked carefully through the pages for some small personal note from Rico. She found it on the back of the last document, written on a yellow Post-it note.

The note read: "Make them protect you."

She rubbed the message he had hand-printed across her cheek and tried to imagine his fingers touching her again. She put the papers back in the mailer and slammed her hand against the roof of her car. Someone had taken him from her, and for that they would pay.

Jasper cocked his head in surprise. He had never seen his mistress get so emotional over the mail before.

Munch drove to the schoolyard but didn't get out right away. She spotted Asia by the jungle gym, surrounded by her group of best friends. Asia was already taller than most of them. Always skinny, her legs had lengthened another inch in the last six months; even her face seemed to have stretched. Soon she would be as tall as Munch, then she would pass her. How weird was that? The little baby Munch had rocked in her arms was closing in on her tween years.

Munch tried to peer into the future, to see the woman Asia would become, but the smoke refused to clear. One thing was certain: The kid was going to be something. She'd been strong-willed from day one, confident and coordinated. One of those kids who led, and others willingly followed.

Asia would be turning heads, Munch was certain of that. Her birth mother's hair had been brown, her daddy's black. Asia's color was a bit of both, a rich brown with some golden highlights from long afternoons in the sun. Even now she ran her fingers through her curls as she talked. Her moves were casually theatrical, and probably unnecessary. She already held her audiences in thrall, whether they were boys or girls. Munch could only pray she would use her powers for good.

Asia also had her daddy to thank for her dark skin, thick lashes and straight nose. She could easily be mistaken as hailing from a number of ethnic groups—Native American, Middle Eastern, Italian, Greek, or Hispanic. If she persisted with her desire to be an actor, her looks would serve her well. Her daddy had been a fine-looking man, a real charmer. If it weren't for his love of dope and his criminal tendencies, he really might have made something of himself. He also might have lived to admire the beautiful kid he had created. Dope and the needle spawned many orphans.

Asia turned and spied Munch. Her expression didn't change, nor her mannerisms. Asia showed the same face to everyone. Munch wondered if that was a privilege of youth—to get to be the same person no matter who you were with.

Asia broke away from her friends and skipped across the parking lot to join her mother. Munch took her schoolbag and threw it in the back seat. Jasper jumped from the back to the front and made whimpering excited noises. Asia held out her face to be licked and the dog obliged.

Asia climbed into the passenger seat and strapped on her seat belt. Jasper settled next to her with a contented sigh and rested his head on her thighs. "You didn't go to work today?" Asia asked.

"No, I had to take care of some things." Munch kissed Asia's cheek and stroked some stray wisps of hair away from the girl's eyes.

"What happened to your face?" Asia asked.

Munch came around to her side and got in. "A cat scratched me."

"We got a cat?" Asia asked excitedly. Jasper lifted his head. The word "cat" was in his vocabulary, probably under the subheading: chew toy.

"No, she was an alley cat."

Asia's expression was critical and slightly disbelieving. "Uh-huh. She must have put up some fight."

Munch checked the scratches again. They *were* a little thick to have been caused by claws. She adjusted her sunglasses and started the car. "So how was school? Did you guys play that math game today?"

"Every Thursday."

"Caroline and Mace invited you to spend the night. They'll take you to school tomorrow and pick you up."

"What about you?"

Munch started the car. "I have some stuff I have to do. I'll see you later at the church."

Asia sat up straighter and her face brightened as if she had suddenly thought of something. "Do you know what I saw at recess?"

“What?”

“A rainbow, only it was round, like a piece of a regular rainbow cut out and pasted to a cloud.”

“Sounds pretty.”

“I think it was Rico and he was waving to me on his way to heaven.”

Munch could only nod, unable to speak for a minute. “Tomorrow, at the mass . . . at St. Monica’s . . .” She stopped and swallowed, blinking back tears. When she spoke again, her voice was thick. “We’ll both get dressed up real pretty and wave back. Okay?”

CHAPTER SEVENTEEN

ELLEN SPENT AN HOUR ON MAKEUP AND CLOTHES. SHE was going for a look that said *I'm not a slut, but I like my fun*. When Humberto arrived at eight that evening, he didn't stand a chance. She was pleased to see he had also taken some extra pains with his appearance. His embroidered guayabera shirt and his slacks were freshly pressed. There was also a shine to his snakeskin boots, and he'd put some product in his hair that tamed his short curls. His forehead was creased with worry lines and his smile wasn't as relaxed as it had been when they met that morning.

"Tough day, honey?" Ellen asked.

"I'm not used to your freeways," he admitted.

"I'm glad you found your way here all right."

He thrust a plastic shopping bag toward her. "This is for you."

"Well, bless your heart." Ellen pulled out the contents, unwrapped the white tissue paper, and saw that he'd brought her a light blue Members Only jacket. The tags were still on the sleeve, but the price had been removed. A lot of men wouldn't think to do that. "Aren't you the sweetest thing."

She took the coat draped over his arm and hung it up in the closet. A quick exploration along the way revealed two sets of keys. One had the car rental company tag, the other (according to the rubber fob) was to a motel in Santa Monica.

He was glancing out her window when she returned to the living room. He gestured around him, taking in the matching furniture, floor-length drapes, and the coffee table with the burl wood base and kidney-shaped glass top. "Nice place."

"Mi casa, su casa," she said. "What can I get you to drink?"

"Coffee."

"I'll be back in a jiff," she said. "Make yourself at home." In the kitchen, Ellen put on the teakettle and wondered if the coffee would be a problem. She knew sodium pentothal dissolved fine in water or alcohol, but she'd never put it into a hot drink. She poured a teaspoon of the yellow crystals into a dark mug. To mask the slight garlic odor of the drug, she sprinkled cinnamon and a tablespoon of cocoa in with the instant coffee granules before adding the hot water.

Humberto stood before her mantel, studying the photographs there. Her mom and stepdad smiled uncertainly from one of the frames. Another picture showed the Colonel in full military uniform.

"That's my daddy," Ellen said, arriving with a tray of cookies and Humberto's coffee. She had made herself tea, just so there was no mixup. "Was my daddy, anyway."

"He has passed away?"

"Him and my mama both. Been about six months now."

"I am sorry for your loss. I am also orphaned."

Ellen set the tray on the coffee table and brought him his cup. She wasn't trying to render the big guy unconscious, more like relaxed. Just a little narcotherapy to loosen his tongue.

He took a sip of his coffee, grimacing slightly. She broke a cookie in two and offered him half. "It's an old family recipe. If you don't like it, it'll just break my heart."

"It's delicious," he lied.

"So, are you just passing through, or are you going to stay awhile?" She gave him her best take-it-any-way-you-want smile.

Color rose to his cheeks. He took a sip a coffee. "I'll probably be here a week, *mas o menos*."

"I hope it's *mas*." She smiled a little more shyly this time. *Mata Hari, eat your heart out.*

He felt a warm glow slip through him and took another sip of the strangely flavored coffee, growing accustomed to its taste.

"Is this your first time in LA?" she asked.

"No, I come here when it is necessary, when my boss sends me for, uh, customer relations. He finds it difficult to travel and I don't mind."

"I love traveling, too," Ellen said. "You hiring?"

"Are you looking for work?"

"Not really. My daddy left me set pretty good." One of Ellen's New Year's resolutions had been to avoid felonies. She had spent enough time in prison to have soured on the whole incarceration experience. Between the death of her parents and the advent of her thirtieth birthday, she was starting to realize that time was too short and too precious to waste.

"Munch might be interested," she said, remembering tonight's mission. "She's always looking to supplement her income, if you know what I'm saying." She reached across him to straighten a picture frame and let a breast brush against his well-muscled arm. Damn, he was solid as a ham hock.

"In our business"—he paused and looked at her—"that would be the cattle business."

She smiled, managing to put a wink in her grin and tone. "Of course. Cows and bulls."

He smiled back, liking her more with each passing moment. "We rely on our agents to handle all business that arises with regards to retail sales, transportation, and issues of security. This leads to problems. It is always difficult when one is unable to personally supervise an operation."

"I can imagine." They had moved to the couch. He was glad. The many events of the day were catching up with him. It felt good to take a moment to relax. Ellen fed him cookies and looked dreamily into his face. She seemed to hang on his every word, as if she cared about him. She blinked her brilliant green eyes, and Humberto was momentarily confused. He remembered brown eyes; perhaps he had been superimposing Ellen and Victoria. No matter, the couch was incredibly comfortable and he had a lightness of being he'd never felt before. Could this be the beginnings of love?

Ellen took a sip of tea. "There's going to be a mass for Rico tomorrow night and then the funeral is Saturday. It's going to be really rough to see Munch so sad."

"Yes, dealing with the family left behind is one of the hardest things I do." Humberto was surprised he had spoken these sentiments out loud. He closed his eyes and saw Felix's face, more specifically the pain in his cousin's eyes. There was never a good way to give such bad news, but perhaps he had been too abrupt. Maybe if he had let some of his own true feelings leak through, shown some empathy, the burden would have been lighter for the sharing. It had been a long time since he stopped and truly looked hard into his own heart. Victoria had pointed this out to him just the other day. He could hear her voice.

"Hey, big boy."

He opened his eyes, momentarily disoriented. It was not Victoria speaking to him now, but this Americana. This Ellen.

"Are you going to sleep on me?" She pouted playfully.

"No." He pulled her to him and kissed her mouth, a little surprised at his own impulsiveness.

She nestled into him, placing her head on his shoulders, and bending her knees so that her feet were tucked under her. "So how long did you know Rico?"

He allowed his hand to rest on her thigh. She didn't object. "I really didn't know him at all. Sometimes I feel as if I don't know anyone." He felt tears fill his eyes, but he wasn't ashamed. This was a breakthrough. And this woman, this beautiful Angeleno, was responsible.

"Oh, pshaw." Ellen kissed him on the cheek and ran a hand across his chest. "I find that hard to believe. You're real easy to talk to and not so bad on the eyes either."

He sighed. "I would have liked to attend university, perhaps studied history."

"I was never much for school," Ellen admitted. "I couldn't get out of my house soon enough."

"I was the oldest son. We were poor. Señor Delaguerra offered me work and I couldn't refuse. I didn't want to refuse. I was the envy of my friends, and soon I could afford many things." He flexed his feet, bringing the toes of his snakeskin boots into view, and stared at them a moment as if he were seeing them for the first time.

Ellen brushed a hand between Humberto's legs. *Holy crap!* she thought, and almost asked him if his first job had been as a mule; he was sure built like one. Probably had some kind of stamina, too. Even with the pentothal lowering his blood pressure, he was already hard enough to get the job done.

She struggled to bring the conversation back on point. "Rico grew up poor, too."

Humberto was not to be drawn away from his self-discovery. "I wouldn't have minded working with my hands. There is no shame in that."

"My friend Munch—" she started to say, but Humberto cut her off before she could finish her sentence.

"People look at me, they see a big man, a frightening man. Señor Delaguerra treats me as if I was another of his pistols, to be aimed and shot at his will, but I'm so much more."

"I'm sure you are." Ellen looked at the clock. He had to be feeling the full effects of the drugs by now. She had expected it to put him out or at least into serious twilight. Obviously, she'd miscalculated his body weight and tolerance. There also, apparently, was no getting him back on the topic of Rico. She kissed him again, this time putting one of his big paws on her breast. He didn't fumble. He was almost too tender.

They necked for another ten minutes, until she inferred that his blood pressure was restored to normal levels.

"Wait a minute," she said.

He stopped. "I'm sorry. Do you want me to leave?"

"Leave?" She almost laughed at his innocence, his old-world manners. "Heavens, no. We're just getting to the good part. C'mon." He staggered a bit when he stood, but quickly recovered.

She led him into her bedroom. He lit the candles by her bed and shut off the light. She started to unbutton her blouse. He stopped her and tilted her face to look up at his. "Are you sure?"

"If you were looking for the Virgin Mary, honey, you came to the wrong cabaña."

His touch lost its gentleness, and Ellen wondered when she had given up control of the evening. The boy wasn't a pistol as much as a rocket, and didn't those blow up sometimes when they were fired?

CHAPTER EIGHTEEN

ON FRIDAY MORNING, ROGER CAME BY MUNCH'S HOUSE AS promised. Or was the correct term "threatened"? He parked out front and let himself in the front gate. Jasper barked nonstop as the cop made his way to her door. By the time he knocked, Jasper's hackles were sticking straight up, and he had assumed the charge position.

"It's okay, boy," Munch said as she opened her door. "I'll take care of this one."

Roger was carrying a briefcase and casing the street with his eyes.

"You look like an insurance salesman," she said.

"I guess I am in a way."

She gestured for him to enter. "I thought we'd do this in the kitchen."

He followed her through her house. Jasper sniffed at his heels, obviously not liking what he was sensing. While she cleared the kitchen table, Roger stooped down and offered his hand. Jasper couldn't be bothered.

"He prefers women," Munch said.

"That's all right, he's just doing his job." Roger set his briefcase on top of the table and clicked it open.

Inside, nestled in gray foam rubber, was a black box the size of a deck of playing cards, an elastic belt with a pocket, and two white cords with black microphones on one end and silver connectors on the other. She reached for the instruction manual, but he stopped her.

"You won't need that; I'll explain everything."

"I figured I'd read along," she said.

"No, I want your full attention." He tucked the manual underneath the padding, then removed the components one at a time. "This is the transmitter." He connected the silver ends of the cords to the black box and inserted it into the belt.

"What's this wire?" she asked.

"The antenna."

She nodded. "Like an AM radio."

"Exactly. You run that up the center of your back. Make sure there's enough slack to compensate for stretching and twisting, but not so much that it might snag on something and get pulled out."

She studied the small wire. "And then I'd stop transmitting?"

"Worse than that. If the antenna wire comes out of its socket, it causes a mismatch at the transmitter and makes it burn out, usually at very high temperatures."

"This would be the thing I'm supposed to strap to my body?"

"Yeah, just be careful with the wire and you shouldn't have any problems. Fit it so the transmitter rides in the small of your back. You could attach the cords and wire with surgical tape, but I use duct tape to be sure."

"Probably less painful to remove duct tape than bullets."

"Exactly."

She watched his face, but there was no change of expression. Either this guy had no sense of humor, didn't get hers, or he had ceased to think of her as a human being and more as another piece of equipment.

He tapped the tiny black microphones at the end of the cords. "And you want the microphones taped to the front of your body, as near your collar as possible without being visible."

She noticed a small black switch on the top of the transmitter. "What's this?"

"That's your on/off switch. The green dot is on, red off. Got that?"

Munch bit back a sarcastic reply. "Yeah, sure."

"Let's run through a test anyway." He walked her to the front window and pointed up the street. "See that white delivery van?"

"Uh-huh." She also noticed that it was the same make and model as the van she and Ellen had seen at Rico's house the first time they'd gone there. Only now the lettering and logo on the door weren't for a locksmith. Now it was a flower delivery van. She wondered if the sign was painted on one of those magnetic mats, such as realtors used on their private cars.

"Detective Chapman is in there with the receiver," Roger said. "Turn your transmitter on."

She toggled the switch to the green position. Roger picked up one of the small black microphones and said, "Flash your lights, Chapman."

The van headlights flicked on and off.

"See?" Roger said. "Child's play."

"Aren't I supposed to get a code word? You know, to tell you guys something's gone wrong?"

"Yeah, sure. What do you want it to be?"

"How about I scream, 'Don't shoot'?"

"Serious?"

Munch sighed. "Oh, forget it. I'll take my chances."

He nodded as if to say: *Suit yourself*. "Wear it to the church this afternoon, just to get the feel of it."

"I don't know about that," Munch said. "A lot of people are going to be hugging me."

"What better test?"

"Okay, fine, but I'm not turning it on."

His face expressed shock at the very suggestion. "Of course not."

She realized she trusted him less when he acted as if he cared.

He closed the briefcase. "When will Asia get home from school?"

There it was again. That familiarity. "I'm having her picked up by some friends, *real* friends. They're going to bring her to the service."

If Roger knew he had been insulted, he didn't show it. Maybe he didn't get emotionally invested when he was working. She imagined he could be anyone he wanted to get the job done. It was a hell of a way to live your life.

After Roger had left, Munch turned on the radio in her bedroom, switching the band to AM so she could listen to the traffic report. There was a sig alert at the airport, heavy traffic on the westbound 10 all the way to the coast, and those planning to traverse the grapevine were advised to bring chains.

She went into the bathroom and started the bathwater, then on to the living room to shut the curtains. The white van had left.

Jasper followed her from room to room whining. She paused to give him her full attention. He'd been neglected of late, perhaps not by most people's scale. She didn't consider him a possession so much as a member of the family. She was also aware how dependent Jasper was on them, and for a lot more than food and water and a place to lift his leg. Jasper had been abandoned by his previous owners and had a lot of emotional neglect to be compensated for. She scratched his throat and the bottom of his chin while he closed his eyes in canine pleasure.

"You didn't like that bad old man," she crooned. "No, you didn't. Mommy didn't either. Who's my good boy?"

Jasper rolled on his back, presenting her with his pee-pee. She scratched his chest, and his legs pedaled the air. *God,* she thought, *what if he died, too?* She couldn't allow herself to think like that. Living things died. That was a fact. With any luck, she'd go first.

"Okay," she said out loud, "that's enough. Mommy needs to get ready." Munch went into the kitchen and collected the transmitter. She strapped the elastic belt around her waist. The ends were Velcro, but not where she needed them to be in order to have a secure fit. Roger should have brought her a petite.

A few well-placed safety pins should do the trick. Her rarely used sewing kit was in her closet. She crossed in front of the radio to get to it and static ensued. Surprised, she checked the transmitter's on/off switch. It was turned to the red. It should have been off. She switched it to the green and the radio still crackled. She moved the transmitter away and the radio broadcast cleared again.

Why, Officer Roger, you little stinker. The switch was a dummy. The transmitter was a continuously live feed. Well, well, well. She was going to have some fun with this.

Victoria Delaguerra picked at the bedcovers and tried not to tap her foot or pull at her lip or any of the hundred other mannerisms Abel knew so well. She didn't know why he was always so suspicious of her. She had never given him cause. None that he knew of, anyway.

He pulled on his black short-sleeved shirt, noticed a thread hanging from one of the buttons and swore.

"I'll fix that," she said, helping him take it off again. She selected a navy blue shirt in the same style, checked to see that it was unflawed, and held it open for him.

"You're being nice," he said.

"I'm sorry I snapped at you yesterday. It must be the moon." She glanced at the clock, trying not to be obvious. Humberto was calling at nine. If Abel answered the phone, Humberto would have no trouble playing the communication off as an update of his mission. Humberto was smart that way, quick on his feet, and sensitive to shifting winds.

This venture was a big opportunity for him. For both of them.

Abel was no fool, Victoria reminded herself. Many other things, but not a fool. If she wanted to hear what progress Humberto was making without her husband around, she needed to act natural.

Mentioning the moon had done the trick. Abel would write her mood off to a woman's thing and be happy to leave.

She really was on a roll lately, though she knew not to let her newfound talent at intrigue go to her head. There was too much at stake to get cocky or careless now.

Still, she thought with no small amount of pride, having the pilot bail just before sending the transport plane into the mountains had been a stroke of genius. Now she and Humberto had the cocaine to convert to cash. Usurping Abel's power structure was going to be as expensive as it was risky. The penalty for failure would be death. The reward for success, huge. The cost of doing nothing, unimaginable.

Victoria blamed Abel for all of it. Would she have been better off if he had not taken her from her home in Colombia? Arguable. Perhaps she would be dead or addicted to the coca leaf as her brothers had been. Perhaps she would have married some peasant, produced baby after baby, and been old and used up before her time. Or maybe she might have found true love and been poor, but happy.

Abel had changed her fate. That much was certain. He had made her a princess, but never a queen. He claimed his marital rights whenever the mood struck him. And he did things to her, odd perverted things she could speak to no one about, not even her priest.

She worried that she was to blame in the beginning. Sex repulsed her, perhaps she was frigid. Then she educated herself, first by reading, then by her own cautious experimentation, and she realized she was not the one at fault. Sex could be wonderful with the right partner. A partner without anal fixations and sadistic perversions.

She did not consider herself a greedy woman, but she was a mother now. She had her children to think of, not to mention the hundred other families that relied on the Delaguerras for their livelihoods. In America, she could claim irreconcilable differences, divorce Abel and receive her rightful half of the estate. But she wasn't in the United States. It was not her fault she had been born on the wrong side of the border.

Abel's escalating volatility and irrationality only fueled her cause. This was a business, and needed to be run with a cool head. Someday he would kill the wrong person and put them all in danger. Perhaps he already had. She hoped to avoid further violence. Civility promoted order. Abel had forgotten that. Violence only begot more violence. Of course, one had to expect a certain amount of blood when pulling a drug cartel coup.

Ellen came by at noon with a black dress for Munch. It was knee-length and properly somber. Munch thanked her while shoving a note in her hand. The note had one simple message: "It's on." Then she parted her robe and showed her friend the contraption strapped to her body.

Ellen didn't miss a beat. "Do you have stockings and black shoes? If not, I could run out and get you some."

"No, I've got those. I would like to borrow your purse." She needed a bag large enough to hold Rico's service revolver. Ellen didn't ask. She dumped the contents of her bag on Munch's bed. Munch handed her a smaller leather purse, taking a moment to marvel at the range of objects Ellen considered crucial enough to keep with her at all times.

Not like the old days, when all they needed was a douche bag, filtered smokes, and a lighter to get them through the cycle of their dope-addicted day. Going from john to cooker, motel room to shooting gallery in a matter of minutes, and stopping at hell and all points in between.

Munch took down the gift-wrapped box from the top shelf of her closet and tore through the paper. Rico's gun was cold when she lifted it from the box. She spun the cartridge chamber, making sure there was a bullet in every slot, and put the weapon in Ellen's purse.

"Make yourself comfortable," she said. "I'm going to take a bath."

"I'll come sit with you."

They left the dress and transmitter in the bedroom, but brought the purse with them into the bathroom. Jasper joined them. Munch had learned from experience that if she excluded Jasper from the room and he could hear her or knew she was in there, he'd claw the paint off the door until she opened it.

"Oh, man," Ellen said, hopping up on the sink counter. "What a night."

Munch checked the bath temperature and adjusted the knobs to add more cold water. "Why? What did you do?"

"What didn't I do? That fella Humberto? Guy's built like a pony. I swear, I about died. I sure enough went to heaven."

"Thanks for making the sacrifice," Munch said wryly. "He tell you anything interesting?"

"He works for some kingpin in Mexico named Señor Delaguerra. I got the impression that he felt underappreciated and was looking to move up."

"Maybe we can use that," Munch said.

Ellen wiped steam from the mirror and checked her makeup. "What's with the wire?"

Munch explained.

"So they don't know you know?"

Munch dropped her robe and stepped into the bath. "That's about the size of it."

"Speaking of size," Ellen said, "Humberto talked in his sleep. He mumbled a few words in Spanish that I didn't quite get."

"Yeah, sometimes that sleep talk is just gibberish, you might catch half a sentence here and there."

"He said a name. Victoria. He said it more than once."

Munch stopped scrubbing her face. Someone named Victoria had signed one of the gushy love cards Rico had hidden under his desk blotter.

Ellen continued, "I asked him this morning who Victoria was and he said, 'Señora Delaguerra?' I said, 'I don't know, sugar, it was your dream.' The boy blushed to his knees."

Munch rinsed off and reached for a towel. "So you think he has a thing for the *Jefe's* wife?"

"That's what it felt like."

"Are you going to see him again?"

Ellen smiled. "I think you can pretty well count on that. He said he'd be in town for a week." She added a layer to her lipstick and pouted at her reflection. "He'll be calling."

"I hope you didn't sleep with him for me," Munch said. She didn't want Ellen giving it up as a first resort.

Ellen looked crestfallen. "I was trying to help."

"I know. I appreciate what you found out. I just don't want you screwing someone because you think you have to. I want you to love yourself more than that."

"Oh," Ellen said. "Good to know." She winked at Munch. "It really wasn't terrible."

"Good. By the way, I'm pretty sure my phone is tapped, too. So think about what you say when you call or leave a message." Munch wrapped a towel around her wet hair, slung the purse strap over her right shoulder, and cinched the robe tightly as she reached for the doorknob. "You ready to mess with big brother?"

"Always."

Jasper seemed to understand them. He went to the door, his forehead almost touching the wood, his eyes watching for the crack to widen so he'd be the first one out.

Munch hesitated, remembering something else she needed to tell Ellen that she wasn't ready to have overheard by the narcs. "Yesterday there were a bunch of scooters across the street visiting my neighbor. A few of the guys were flying Satan's Pride colors."

"Did you recognize any of them?" Ellen asked.

"No, and they seemed oblivious of the house."

"Still," Ellen said, "it's probably only a matter of time before your name gets dropped or the wrong guy recognizes you."

"Yeah, that's what I was thinking. I can't call the cops. That would just make it worse."

"You could move," Ellen said.

Munch felt a gust of righteous anger. She was well on a spiritual path, doing everything she was supposed to; why was she getting penalized for being the law-abiding one? "Fuck that shit. I own this house. I'm not going to pick up and scurry off every time a chopper comes down the street."

"So what *is* the play?"

"I want you to get a message to Petey for me. Tell him I've got some information for him. I'll meet him in public somewhere. Tell him it's worth his while."

"You got it," Ellen said.

"Thanks." She opened the bathroom door and mouthed to Ellen, "It's show time."

PART THREE
JUSTICE FOR ALL

CHAPTER NINETEEN

HUMBERTO PARKED THE RENTAL CHEVY ON THE STREET. The motel had parking in the back, but he had already taken the only empty slot for his 1985 Silverado short-bed pickup truck. The red soil of Mexico still clung to the undersides of the fenders. He'd driven the rig hard to get here so quickly. Flying would have been faster, but had been out of the question, especially with what he carried.

When this was over, he would splurge on a thorough detail, inside and out. He tried to be modest, but seemed to lose all control when it came to his cherished truck. Despite himself, he loved the way the teenage boys stared with unabashed envy when he cruised the main boulevards and how the smaller boys ran alongside him in heavy traffic, shouting with excitement, knowing better than to touch.

The headers and the glass packs on his straight pipes created a mighty roar and heralded the power of his big V-8 engine. Three hundred and fifty cubic inches of get up and go. When he took to the highway and opened it up, his hand on the leather-covered steering wheel and boot on the gas pedal, the window rolled down so that the air rushing past filled his ears, it was as if he and the ride were one.

He also took great pride in the cosmetic flourishes: the custom paint job, the Brahma bull horns affixed to the hood, and the center-line rims. The truck was one of a kind and bore scant resemblance to the model he'd bought new, with cash money, off the showroom floor.

His coat pockets bulged with quarters, and the sunlight burned his eyes. He blamed the smog. How did the people of Los Angeles tolerate it?

The pay phone outside the motel was near a bus bench. An older man in even older army fatigues sat there, well within hearing. Humberto walked to the corner. He had spotted a bank of phones mounted outside a small convenience store. Three were missing the hand receivers, but the fourth was operational.

He punched in the numbers from memory, then deposited twice as many quarters as the operator requested so there would be no interruptions. The phone rang twice.

"Bueno." Victoria sounded out of breath.

"Is Señor Delaguerra there?" Humberto asked.

She switched to English. "No, he left thirty minutes ago. How's it going?"

"Okay. I've contacted Enrique's women."

"More than one?"

"Christina and a *gavacha* named Munch who claims they were getting married. Chicken said he'd seen her with Enrique."

"Any problems?"

"They both want a cut."

Victoria clicked her tongue. "Greedy bitches."

Humberto let that assessment pass without further comment. "And the *Jefe?*"

"He is angry. He knows someone has betrayed him."

"I'll take care of that," Humberto said. "Meanwhile, I have found our first buyer. Don't worry, *querida mia,* everything is going to work out." Hc hung up, and the pay phone saw fit to return all his money. He took this as a good sign.

He went inside the store, bought a cup of coffee, a bar of chocolate, a large bag of chips, and asked the clerk to double-bag his purchases. He slipped a quarter into the newspaper vending machine on the corner, opening the glass front when he heard the click of the latch releasing. He only took one copy of the *LA Times,* although he easily could have taken them all, but he was not a greedy man, nor a dishonest man when he could avoid it.

With the cup of coffee in one hand, his bag of groceries in the other, and the newspaper tucked under his arm, Humberto walked back to the motel by way of the alley. He saw no one, but to be safe he walked past his truck the first time, then turned and walked past it again. Satisfied that nobody was lurking nearby observing him, he unlocked the passenger door and slid across the tooled-leather bench seat. He slid the key in the ignition and turned it counterclockwise to the accessory position. Two red lights illuminated on the instrument panel. He simultaneously pushed the third and fifth buttons on the radio and a panel dropped open beneath the glove box. He removed two brick-sized bundles wrapped in brown paper. A dancing skeleton was stamped in black ink over the folds on the side. He would leave the wrapping intact. The skeleton stamp was testimony to the cocaine's quality. Inside the brown paper, the drugs were protected by another layer of foil that covered a third layer of plastic wrap. Each bundle weighed a kilo. The cocaine within was ninety-eight percent pure and had a street value of thirty-five thousand dollars in its current form—a steal at his asking price of twenty-five grand.

Humberto didn't have the time to hold out for top dollar or the connections to cut and break down the coke to smaller, more valuable, weight. He needed big money and a swift liquidation. In a week's time, he required large sums of cash for bribes, especially if he was going to outbid Abel Delaguerra for the loyalty of the regional general. The countdown had begun.

The secret compartment under the dashboard held ten more packages of product. Twenty additional bricks were secreted in the independently sealed bottom half of the gas tank behind the seat. Selling the entire shipment at once to a single buyer would bring unwanted attention. The gossip generated by such a transaction would surely reach the ears of Señor Delaguerra and the other cartel bosses. Humberto was counting on the advantage of surprise.

He would make Enrique's women earn their money before he decided their ultimate fate. If he wasn't able to raise the cash he needed, he couldn't come back to the ranch empty-handed. Delaguerra suspected a traitor, and would not be happy until one was delivered and an example made.

Humberto put the two bricks of coke in the grocery bag under the bag of chips, pushed the secret compartment shut again, and returned to his motel room. His bulky coat with its many straps and buckles was already laid out across his bed. The lining of the pockets unsnapped and revealed two netted slings. He removed the automatic weapons hidden there and replaced them with the kilos.

He was all set, even ahead of schedule. Humberto took a sip of his coffee, unfolded the morning's newspaper, and turned to Enrique Chacón's obituary. The survivors were listed in order of importance to the deceased. First came the father, then the daughter, the fiancée, the siblings, the ex-wife, and then on to the extended family: aunts and uncles; nieces and nephews. Chacón would serve well as the scapegoat. Suspicions about his loyalty had already been raised. And although he'd proved himself in the end, there might still be enough embers of suspicion lingering that could be fanned into flame. Humberto would have to come up with a creative explanation for his death at the hands of American police, fighting side by side with the Santiago brothers.

Abel Delaguerra would not lower his guard until the traitor was revealed and his or her family eliminated. None of that would be necessary, of course, if Humberto could raise the capital he needed; then what Abel Delaguerra did or didn't want would be a moot point.

He toyed with the idea of telling Christina this. Enrique's Mexican lover had already assured him she had the connections to move two kilos, perhaps more. If she knew her life depended on it, she might be more motivated. The same with Munch, although he hadn't approached her yet.

His budding relationship with Ellen complicated things. Without conscious thought, his hand moved to his dick. He rubbed himself and thought of the nimble American. They had screwed each other unconscious, and he had slept like a dead man after. Just what the doctor ordered.

He wondered what he had been dreaming to call out Victoria's name. He had allowed the *Jefe*'s wife to believe he was caught up in her charms. Once upon a time this had been true, but things changed, fires cooled. He was adept at keeping his true feelings private. And she in turn had been conceited enough to believe that a man would risk his life for a chance to get between her sheets. As if he could ever trust a woman who would betray the father of her children.

He sighed, feeling a melancholy twinge for the old days.

The narco business used to be fun as well as lucrative. There was plenty for everyone. When he was *Jefe,* he would remember his roots. He would throw grand parties with music and dancing. Orphans would be invited. Everyone would be invited. They would eat and drink until their bellies could hold no more. *Corridos* would be written and sung to honor the rising of a new and just overseer. A man of the people and for the people, that would be his legacy.

Humberto had no aspirations to sit on a throne, to be the "king of the white powder," as Abel Delaguerra had dubbed himself.

The Delaguerras had both gotten drunk on the same power, and neither of them understood the real issue. Nobody has control over the drug business. Not the traffickers nor the generals nor the police of any country. Demand controlled the business. The best one could do was to service that demand, enjoy the bounty, and leave the glory to God.

But first things first. Humberto finished his coffee. He mugged for the mirror above his dresser, smiling and glowering in turn. Although he probably wouldn't need his pistols, leaving them behind was also out of the question. His boots made good temporary holsters, especially with the help of the elastic bands stitched on the inside. He put on his coat and went out front to where he had parked his disappointing rental Chevy. At least the manufacturers hadn't made the door panels any more difficult to pry open. He made a note to pick up a screwdriver, squeezed behind the wheel of the Monte Carlo, and went on to his assignation with Christina.

While waiting for the mourners to arrive, Munch read the plaques on the sacristy's walls. Ellen joined her at the statue of Saint Monica. The statue was carved from white marble. Saint Monica's head, encased in what looked like a nun's wimple, was canted downward and the expression on her chiseled face was both sad and sweet.

Ellen picked up a card with another depiction of the saint on the front. This time, Monica was seated, still wearing a wimple. There was an open book on her lap and a shepherd's crook in one hand. A halo circled behind her head and a single tear emerged from one eye. "What are these?" Ellen asked. "Catholic trading cards?"

"Something like that," Munch said, taking the holy card from Ellen and flipping it over.

"Widow," the card read.

God, Munch thought, *there was no escaping this shit*.

She read aloud, "Born of Christian parents at Tagaste, North Africa, in 333; died at Ostia, near Rome, in 387. Married to Patritius, who held an official position in Tagaste. Mother of Augustine. Patritius was a pagan."

"You'd think they'd've discussed that shit before they got married," Ellen said. "I didn't know the Pagans had been around that long. I wonder what kind of Harley Patritius rode."

Munch looked at Ellen in mock astonishment. "I was wondering the exact same thing."

"See? There you go."

Munch read on. " 'Monica was not the only matron in Tagaste whose married life was unhappy, but, by her sweetness and patience, she was able to set an example in her village.' "

"Some example," Ellen said. "What was she? The patron saint of co-dependents?"

Munch scanned to the bottom. "Close. Prayers are said to her on behalf of abuse victims, alcoholics, and—get this—'sons and husbands who have gone astray.' Should we light a candle?"

"Yeah, sure. The question is whose ass to hold it to. By the way, I told that guy Humberto that you might be interested in supplementing your income."

"How'd that come up?" Munch asked.

"He asked me if I might be looking for work. I'm told him no. But then I was thinking about how you said we were going to help the police get to the bottom of Rico's murder—uh, shooting."

Munch smiled at the "we."

"I got the distinct impression that Humberto was suggesting something illegal. Now you know I've gone straight, just like you, but Humberto doesn't know that."

"Thanks. I'll tell the cops, see how they want to handle it."

"Don't mention it; you know the only reward I want is to see justice served."

Munch frowned at Ellen. She was starting to lay it on a bit thick.

Their conversation was cut short by the arriving guests. And not a moment too soon.

Munch left the private sanctuary and took her place with Fernando at the large engraved wooden front door of the chapel. Fernando shook hands, while Munch accepted hugs and kisses on her cheeks. The mortuary had provided a guest book for the mourners to sign. An usher in a dark suit made sure everyone found a seat.

Two network news satellite trucks set up across the street. Munch recognized a woman reporter who was performing a sound check and directing her cameramen to shoot background footage of the church and black-clad mourners.

Ellen planted herself in the front pew, next to Munch and Asia.

The open coffin was displayed up front, behind the railing where the faithful accepted communion and below the priest's pulpit. Flower arrangements and wreaths on easels filled the air with a sweet perfume. Munch wondered if the smell of flowers would now be forever ruined for her.

She leaned over to Asia. "You don't have to go up there and look if you don't want to. It's not him anymore."

Asia's eyes were wide and solemn. "Are you going to go?"

"Yes."

"Then I will, too."

Munch felt an enormous wave of pride for her brave and empathic daughter. She squeezed the little girl's hand. "Thank you."

There was an anticipatory rustle in the room as Father Lanning, in full white robes, swept down the aisle. He paused to take Fernando's hand and murmur something that made Fernando nod in agreement. Father Lanning then laid a hand on Cruz's head and smiled beatifically. Cruz smiled back, childlike, an echo of the emotions surrounding him. Father Lanning continued down the front row. Sylvia crossed herself. Angelica wouldn't meet his eye. He seemed accepting of the teenager's reaction.

At last he came to Munch and Asia and Ellen.

He looked Munch in the eye and said, "God didn't bring you this far to drop you."

Munch felt a tingling sensation climb up her back to her scalp. She didn't go in for all the mumbo-jumbo of organized religion, but she recognized when God reached out and spoke to her directly.

She managed to mumble back, "I know that." And she did know that, though not lately. She'd forgotten lots of things she knew. That was a common denominator among alcoholics and addicts, sober or not. They were the last to remember and the first to forget. It was these timely reminders, delivered by angels of all ilks, that she counted as miracles.

It was also at that moment, with the smell of incense and flowers in her nose, the sun filtering in through panes of colored glass, the church bells striking the hour, that she knew she needed to find a way to get through this. And she knew why. It was for Asia and Angelica, to lead by example. Survival wasn't for wimps.

Father Lanning mounted the stairs to his pulpit and intoned, "Let us pray."

The service went on with the liturgy. Father Lanning's voice was sonorous and hypnotic. The church was warm. Munch stared at the open casket. They'd done a nice job of cleaning Rico up. His mouth was closed and there was a faint suggestion of a smile on his lips as if he were sleeping peacefully. The skin color was more natural and they must have put some padding under his—

Rico's eyelids fluttered. Munch bolted upright as terror shot through her. She sneaked a look sideways at the other mourners, waiting for someone else to scream first.

Get a grip, she told herself. This wasn't some horror movie. He'd been shot, autopsied, and embalmed. No one could survive all that. It was an illusion of light combined with fatigue. It was the candle-lights that flickered, not his eyes.

Ellen reached over and squeezed Munch's hand. Asia snuggled into her, finding the comforting softness of her mother's breast. As she cuddled, Asia also sucked the three middle fingers of her right hand, as she used to do when she was a toddler.

Munch took a deep breath and noticed that Father Lanning was finished with his sermon and stepping down. A plump, mustached Hispanic politician who was some representative of something or on the board of something replaced the priest. Munch didn't quite catch or understand his relevance to her life or Rico's. The guy started speaking about the Hispanic community and role models. His self-serving speech was so permeated with ambiguity as to be impossible to understand in any language.

"And so it begins," Munch said under her breath.

Ellen leaned over and whispered in her ear, "What do they call four Mexicans in a boat full of holes?"

"I give up," Munch whispered back.

"Quattro sinko."

Munch strangled back a laugh. Fucking Ellen. She buried her face in Ellen's shoulder, hoping that her heaving shoulders would be interpreted as sobs. Asia pulled her fingers from her mouth and patted Munch's leg. Her mouth dropped open in astonishment when she realized that the two adult women above her were laughing.

"Stop it," she hissed. "You're humiliating me."

This only made them laugh harder. Ellen buried her face in her hands. Munch stopped looking at her until she could get herself under control. She kissed the top of Asia's head. "I'm sorry, honey."

Hands patted her shoulders and she turned back to smile her appreciation. What she saw was Mace and Caroline St. John; her boss Lou; her sponsor Ruby; Happy Jack—her boss when she first got sober—and his wife; Art Becker and his wife; even Cassiletti, Mace's protégé, who had brought a date. The row behind them was filled with the other guys from work and four women Munch sponsored. She didn't know how they knew to come. It certainly wasn't expected of them, but it was very thoughtful, particularly for the newly sober whose heads weren't out of the dryer yet.

What she felt was loved. She'd forgotten how this worked that the worst moments of her life were always balanced somehow with the best of human nature.

She felt the microphone jab into her collarbone and wondered what Roger and Chapman were making of all this.

CHAPTER TWENTY

HUMBERTO DROVE TO CHRISTINA'S APARTMENT. NUMBER 6, she had told him, on the second floor. He could park in the back if he liked. He wouldn't and he didn't.

He arrived for their meeting a half hour early, and did some re-con. Her apartment had a front and a back door. Unusual for an upper-floor unit. She had only told him about the front entrance. The back door he discovered on his own when he walked the perimeter. The door was the type that had a window built into it. A dryer vent protruded to the left of the door. Wooden stairs on the right led down to the driveway and parking for the building.

The driveway was shaped like a flag, with the pole running the length of the building and opening to a paved rectangle painted with yellow lines. The spaces were numbered one to seven. A blue Honda Civic with primer spots occupied Christina's space. He put his hand on the hood. It was slightly warm. The other slots were mostly va-cant. Splatters of various automobile fluids glistened on the cracked asphalt assigned to apartments 4, 5, and 7.

Weeds grew in the cracks under an aged Oldsmobile up on blocks. A boat in a rusted trailer was parked beside the Olds. It, too, had seen better days.

There was a string of free-standing garages at the far end of the parking lot and no alley. Most of the garages were padlocked. One door had a red-and-white FOR RENT sign tacked to it.

His car was parked at the curb, and would remain there. He

rubbed his arms as if suddenly realizing he was cold, and retrieved his coat from the trunk. A car drove by and he glanced at it briefly, avoiding eye contact with the driver. The car was a dark blue Ford, the driver a lone white man. There had been a yellow parking stub under the passenger-side windshield wiper. All this he had noted in a second's time.

Humberto wondered what the driver of the Ford had thought of him. Probably nothing. Humberto was just another big dumb Mexican after all. He shifted the gun in his right boot so that the barrel rested to the side of his ankle and crossed the sidewalk.

The building's scrappy front lawn was more weeds than grass, but trimmed short. A few shrubs with dusty leaves and a twin palm shared the same flower bed. The cement stairs leading to the second-floor landing were flanked with iron railings in need of paint.

Apartment 6 was a corner unit. He knocked on the green wooden door, placing his face in front of the peephole. The mini blinds to his left parted briefly. Moments later, the new-looking dead bolt snicked open.

"Aye, yi yi," he said.

Both of Christina's eyes were black and swollen. She lifted the ice bag she was holding to her lip long enough to say, "Come in."

He stuck his head in the door and looked quickly left and right.

"We're alone," she said. She tossed the ice bag into a large ceramic ashtray.

He sat on the couch and rubbed his palms across the tops of his thighs. "Are we set?"

She licked her lips and winced. "They wanted me to test a sample."

Humberto scratched his shin, feeling the reassuring pressure of his forty-five. "Who?"

"The guys putting up the money."

She went into the kitchen and returned with a paper sack and a small plastic box. He recognized the logo on the box. It was a Ferguson Test Kit. She opened the paper bag to show him the stacks of bills.

She removed a vial of pink fluid from the test kit. "Do you have it?"

He reached in his pocket and removed a brick of dope, setting it on the coffee table next to the cash.

She straightened a paper clip and broke open the vial. Pointing toward the coke, she asked, "Do you mind?"

"Please," he said, his ears cocked for any sound that didn't belong in the supposedly empty apartment. Christina looked older to him than he had first thought. She was probably in her thirties rather than her twenties. Her businesslike manner brought this to his attention. His reevaluation was reinforced as he studied her face more closely. Now he noticed the creases in her forehead and the hardness in her eyes. His attention hadn't been focused on her face the first time they had met.

She stabbed through the wrapping and then dipped the cocaine-powdered end of the bent paper clip into the pink solution. The test fluid turned robin's-egg blue. She smiled lopsidedly. "I think I'm in love."

They made the exchange. He didn't need to count the money there. He flipped through the stacks, making sure they were all American bills. He would count the money later, in private. If the count was short, well . . . He was reasonably sure she knew better.

"How do I get ahold of you?" she asked.

"Chicken knows how to reach me. Call him."

Humberto took a circuitous route back to the motel, retrieved three more packages from his truck, and went to the house on Hampton. Chicken was waiting for him out front, nervously hopping from one foot to the next, scratching the dirt at his feet. Humberto wondered if this was how he had earned his nickname.

Chicken got in the Chevy and directed Humberto to a house in Compton. They drove down Rosecrans, a wide avenue in the predominantly black neighborhood. The liquor stores offered to cash checks and decorated their windows with Laker pennants. The small markets accepted food stamps and sold lottery tickets. Humberto wondered if they made direct exchanges. Girls in knee-high boots and short skirts waited at bus stops, but judging by the way they assessed the single-occupant males of passing cars, it was not for public transportation.

"What do you think, *esse?*" Chicken asked, giving the nod to a chubby black woman in hot pants and a red wig. "You want to change your luck?"

"My luck is running well," Humberto said.

"Okay, turn up here," Chicken said, giving thc hooker an apologetic shrug, which she answered with a one-fingered salute. Chicken glowered at the disrespect. "I ought to go back and cut that *puta* a new hole."

"She's lucky we have other things to do," Humberto said, reasonably certain that the amply endowed prostitute could take Chicken one-handed. He knew girls like her, girls who concealed razors in their hair or stilettos in their boots and would just as soon slice you as spit on you. At least this one was open about her hostility. He appreciated honesty in women.

They pulled up to a house on a side street. Three teenage kids with very black skin sat on the front stairs. Rap music drummed from a boom box at their feet. Two of the boys wore their hair long and natural, with metal "cake cutter" pick combs stuck in the sides. Humberto thought again of the hooker, open hostility, and concealed weapons. The third boy wore a hair net and recognized Chicken with a nod. A jet took off overhead, drowning out the music. The two long-haired boys bobbed their heads, keeping the beat perfectly until the jet had passed.

"This guy is cool," Chicken said to Humberto as he returned the teenager's nod. "The father might be there, Walter. He's the bank."

"How does he make his money?" Humberto asked.

"*Chiva*. Lamont, that's the kid in the hair net, thinks the future is in blow. He talks a lot, but these guys are solid."

Humberto nodded in acknowledgment, but not agreement. From what he knew of the narco business, and that was considerable, he didn't think heroin would ever go out of fashion.

The teenagers parted, creating a narrow path for Humberto and Chicken. Lamont knocked on the door, two quick taps, a pause, then two more, and then he invited them to follow him in. The television was on and tuned to a soap opera. Seated on a plush orange couch opposite the set was a very fat black man. A thin white woman with a bad complexion and unfocused eyes sat beside him stroking his head. Another girl, much younger, but with dark circles under her glassy pale blue eyes rubbed lotion into the big man's hands.

"I love your skin, baby," she said. She sounded sincere.

"You'll forgive me if I don't get up," the fat man said.

"I wouldn't either," Humberto said. He watched the television show for a minute, mesmerized by the flashing dark eyes of a beautiful woman who was obviously up to no good. It amused him that outlaws followed the trials and tribulations of wealthy socialites with the same fascination that the law-abiding set had for shows about cops and robbers.

Chicken waited for the commercial, then planted himself in front of the television. "Walter, this is my homeboy, Humberto." The younger woman's blouse was carelessly buttoned, but Chicken ignored the free show.

Lamont had gone into another room and now returned carrying a long flat wooden box with an electrical cord which he plugged into a wall socket. Chicken, Humberto, and Lamont all sat down around a glass-topped table. Humberto noticed the multiple straight scratches left by single-edge razor blades. Lamont opened the hinged box to reveal a red, LED, digital display crystal, a one-by-two-inch stainless-steel rectangle, various knobs, and a compartment full of glass slides.

"Let's see the shit," Lamont said.

The girl on the couch raised her head as if she were a Labrador retriever and someone had just said, "Ball."

Humberto put a kilo on the table. Lamont opened one end. The inside of the paper wrapping had a number on it: 249. Humberto hid his discomfort. He didn't know the bundles were numbered. This could be a problem.

Lamont put a small amount of the cocaine on one of the glass slides and chopped it up very fine. He put the slide on the rectangle of steel inside the box and flipped a switch. The LED display, which had been blinking dashes, showed the temperature in Fahrenheit degrees.

"This'll take a few minutes to get going," Lamont said. He spooned a second small helping of cocaine into a petri dish, again crushing the crystals into a fine powder. While he worked, he chanted a steady monologue, directed at no one, under his breath.

Both women were now looking at them. The younger one licked her lips.

Lamont poured some methanol into the dish with the cocaine and swirled it around.

"What's you doing now, boy?" Walter asked.

Lamont showed him. "I'm looking for complete solubility."

Walter laughed. "Yeah, so's Marjorie here." He slapped the older woman on her bare thigh, and she laughed indulgently.

Several minutes passed. The heating element on the hot box glowed red. The display showed 150 degrees Fahrenheit. Lamont's chanting became a song.

Marjorie untangled herself from the couch and came over to watch. "Looking good, Daddy," she said. "Looking real good."

Humberto was unconcerned. The common cuts used to dilute

coke were sugar-based and would leave golden-brown dots of caramelization when heated. He knew his cocaine was pure. It would melt cleanly and quickly at 198 degrees. He admired Lamont's professionalism. Chicken could learn a thing or two.

Lamont looked at Marjorie. "Okay, girl, get your stuff."

Marjorie went into the bathroom and returned with a glass of water and a zippered leather kit, such as one might keep manicure tools in. She opened the kit to reveal a syringe and spoon. Lamont measured a quarter gram into her spoon, saying, "The proof of the pudding . . ."

Marjorie finished his sentence, ". . . is in the tasting." She drew water into the syringe and slowly squeezed it into the bowl of the spoon. The white crystals dissolved quickly. She dropped a small wad of cotton into the solution and drew the liquid cocaine back into the syringe through this makeshift filter.

They waited while she found a vein and slammed the coke directly into her bloodstream. A smile formed on her lips and she seemed to be in the throes of an orgasm.

"It's good?" Lamont asked needlessly.

"Oh, yeah. It's very good."

Lamont lifted his shirt to reveal a money belt and counted out the cash. "Give me a day or two to talk to some of my boys, and we can move some serious weight."

"You got it, my brother," Chicken said.

Mutually lucrative business transactions, Humberto noted, made brothers of them all.

Ten minutes later, Chicken and Humberto were out the door.

Christina had also noticed that the kilos of cocaine were numbered. She unfolded the end flap and positioned the packages on the front page of a week-old copy of the the *LA Times*. She took many Polaroids, making sure in the last few that the three-digit numbers, the black ink skeletons, and the headline with last week's date all showed plainly.

She'd also seen Chacón's obituary, read it as she ran her tongue along the inside of her split lip. Stupid little bitch had provided a shopping list of Rico's entire family. Fucking amateurs.

CHAPTER TWENTY-ONE

ELLEN HAD ARRANGED FOR MUNCH TO MEET WITH PETEY on Saturday afternoon. First Munch had to get through Rico's funeral on Saturday morning. She wasn't worried about her safety. She would be in the company of hundreds of policemen.

At nine A.M., the only bikers visible were the rows of motorcycle cops accompanying the hearse that delivered Rico's body to the Holy Cross Cemetery in Culver City.

Munch had her limo bring her and Asia. They had stopped at Fernando Chacón's house in Lawndale on the way and picked up Fernando, Sylvia, and Angelica. These were all the people closest to Rico as far as Munch knew.

As far as she knew, which wasn't far enough, apparently.

Rico once said most wives of undercover officers didn't want detailed accounts of what their spouses did while on the job. Munch had been the opposite. She often was. Rico had chosen to hold back on her. It was for her own good, he said, and at the time she had believed him.

At the time.

There it was again. She hated how doubt had crept into her thoughts.

It was a bright clear cold day. Snow capped the San Gabriel Mountains visible to the north. The mayor was there, as were several city council members, the city attorney, and the Los Angeles County District Attorney, putting on a show for the troops. Munch wouldn't have known any of them if she had tripped over them. Well, maybe the mayor.

The day passed in a blur of politicos shaking her hand without looking at her, but making sure they faced the camera. Art Becker wept openly, unconcerned about how it might look. She saw several photographers record his grief.

A semicircle of folding chairs had been assembled at graveside. Rico's academy graduation photo had been enlarged to poster size and placed on an easel next to the tarp-covered waiting grave. He looked young and strong. For the photograph he had affected a fierce glare. He was also wearing a wedding band. Munch thought about his life when this picture was snapped. Rico would have had a new wife and baby girl at home to feed, his career before him, his early years of poverty in Mexico in the past.

Munch studied Sylvia now, standing stoically in a large black hat. Angelica was even paler than usual, no small feat. Sylvia, seeming to have sensed Munch's scrutiny, turned to her. Fresh tears streaked her face. Munch gestured to the open chairs, inviting Sylvia to make peace. Sylvia grabbed her daughter's arm and led her to the front row. Asia reached out a hand to Angelica. After a moment's hesitation, Angelica took the small hand, offered so guilelessly, and sat.

Munch looked for Fernando and found him within a knot of his other sons. The siblings formed a protective ring around the grieving patriarch, and now moved en masse to the folding chairs.

She somehow sat through another hour of speeches. Dark glasses hid her eyes as she summoned her own memories of her beloved.

Asia had picked a bouquet from their yard and clutched it to her chest as she listened to all the words being said. When the last politicians finally ran out of wind, she carefully unwrapped the foil, packed with wet paper towels, and distributed roses to the women around her.

And a child shall lead them, Munch thought.

A bugle played taps. The family stood and filed past the sealed casket. The women placed their flowers on the grass beneath Rico's portrait, and then negotiated the soft turf to the waiting cars.

During the drive back to Fernando's, nobody spoke. Asia fell asleep on Angelica's lap and had to be roused gently when the limo pulled up in front of the house in Lawndale.

"Are you coming in?" Sylvia asked.

Munch looked closely at Sylvia, waiting for the left-handed comment, the implied insult, that Rico's ex-wife was so wont to dish out. This time, she seemed to be saying exactly what she meant. Though not exactly a warm invitation, coming from Sylvia the question was tantamount to rolling out the red carpet.

"Maybe later. I was hoping to go home, maybe catch a nap."

"Asia can come with us if she wants," Angelica said.

Munch was flabbergasted. Both for the invitation and that Angelica was capable of unprompted social overtures. Not to mention expressing a sentiment that didn't revolve around her.

Munch turned to her daughter. "Up to you."

"I'd like to go with them," Asia said. "You're coming back, right?"

"Of course I am."

Angelica put a protective, if bone-thin, arm around Asia's shoulders. "I'll take care of her."

Munch kissed her daughter good-bye, gave the driver his instructions, and then sat back for the ride home to Santa Monica. Back into the belly of the beast, as it were.

Munch met with Petey at the coffee shop on Pico and Lincoln. It was close enough to the police station to ensure at least one party of cops would be there, off-duty or in uniform. She took a booth by the window that cast plenty of light on their table. Petey swaggered in at the appointed hour. He probably assumed that she had asked for this meeting so she could beg for her life or buy him off somehow. She was really going to enjoy watching the smirk leave his face.

"Hello, Munch," he said, swinging into his seat, chains jangling. He smelled of tobacco and stale beer and unwashed hair. She also detected garlic on his breath and that from all the way across the table from him. He wasn't half as cute as she remembered. Funny how things changed once the veil of intoxication was lifted.

"Hello, Petey," she said. "They still calling you that?"

"Yeah." His expression was suspicious.

"Oh, I'm sorry, I had heard different."

Now he was getting mad. "What did you hear?"

"Something about a desert fox." She opened her purse. "Let me look it up. I want to make sure I get it right."

Sweat broke out on Petey's forehead and he looked as if he might be sick.

She pulled out one of the many copies of the forms Rico had mailed her and spread them across the surface of the table. "Here's the deal. I've sent copies to different friends."

"What do you want?" Petey asked, his voice sort of a croak.

"I want you to live a long and healthy life. Just like me. You're my new guardian angel." She wrote her address on the back of one of the forms. "This is where I live. I work in Brentwood, at that Texaco station. If my friends hear something has happened to me, and only if, copies of these papers will be sent to Tony Martin. You know the name, right? He's the Mongols' lawyer. I also have left instructions that Red Al gets this information. He's still in San Quentin, right?"

"You know he is," Petey said.

"I bet he's good and pissed."

"Okay, I get your point. You don't have to worry about us anymore."

"You got one of those courtesy cards with you?" Munch asked. Courtesy cards were what bikers passed out in lieu of business cards, but they were more than that. They had the club logo, the name of the club member who had issued it, and a space to write in the recipient's name. The bearer was officially a friend of the club. On the rare times a woman had one, it could very well serve as a "get out of hell free" card. She had him fill it out to Miranda "Munch" Mancini. "Date it today," she added.

One down, Munch thought, a million to go. But all she could do was all she could do. One asshole at a time.

CHAPTER TWENTY-TWO

ABEL DELAGUERRA PACED HIS FLOOR AND STARED AT nothing. He didn't like the reports he was getting. An unaccounted-for kilo of his cocaine, displaying the revered black skeleton, had shown up in Los Angeles. Was this a counterfeit? The work of some narco pirate infringing on his hard-won trademark? Or was this part of the shipment he had lost to thieves in the mountains?

The tip had come from that Peruvian woman, *La Sombra,* she was called. The Shadow. She was a freelancer whose services were available to the highest bidder. She brokered many things: information, weapons, airplanes, disappearance services. The tantalizing snippet of information had come in the form of a Polaroid photograph, passed to him by a young child who said only that a lady in a black veil had given him two Hershey bars to deliver it. When pressed, the child admitted that they were the kind with the nuts.

The picture showed a sealed kilo of his product placed strategically on the front page of last Friday's *Los Angeles Times.* On the back of the photo was a phone number with a Los Angeles area code. *Saturday, noon,* it read, *if you're curious.* The note was signed with an *S* that appeared to be casting a shadow. *La Sombra*'s mark.

At exactly twelve o'clock he placed the call.

La Sombra answered her phone with a curt "*¿Sí?*"

"It's Señor Delaguerra," he said in Spanish. "Returning your call."

"Good morning, sir. What is your pleasure?"

He liked her manners. Deadly and polite, always a winning combination. "I understand you have located a book for me. One I am most anxious to have back in my collection."

"Yes," she said, toying with her crescent-moon earring, "I thought you might be interested. How have you been? I haven't gotten a letter from you in a long time."

"I will send you twenty-five thousand letters if I could restore my library."

"I hope they will be in American. I'm trying to improve my English."

He chuckled. "Of course." Twenty-five thousand pesos would buy several nice dinners in Los Angeles. Twenty-five thousand American dollars would feed a small village in Mexico for a year. "Is there a mark on the inside cover?" he asked.

"There is. I would be happy to send you another photograph. Perhaps you could post a letter to me outlining our agreement."

So it was to be cash and carry. This was a problem. Abel hated to wait, but in such an uncertain world, cash was king. They both understood that. "I am a man of my word," he said.

"I am not saying otherwise, but I have expenses to cover. I'm sure you understand. If you are in a big hurry, perhaps you can come over for the day. The weather is beautiful now."

"Not too hot?"

"No, very pleasant."

Abel sipped his hot chocolate and struggled to keep the agitation out of his voice. *La Sombra* had strict rules regarding whom she would deal with, especially on a face-to-face basis. Humberto was already there, but he might as well be in Canada. *La Sombra* would never agree to meet with a middleman. In any case, Abel didn't want to divert Humberto's attention from his appointed task. The big man's job was equally important and possibly connected to the errant product, which was all the more reason to keep Humberto unaware of this latest twist.

Part of Abel's strength was that no one person was privy to all his moves.

He sighed into the phone. "Could I talk you into coming to me? I would, of course, pay all your expenses."

"Regretfully, this is a busy time for me. Let me see if I can move some dates on my calendar. I will call you later. Shall we say five?"

"Thank you, señorita, I will be most anxious to hear from you. Please inform me immediately if you run across any more books and I will really make your trip worthwhile."

"I'm sure you will." Christina smiled as she hung up the phone.

When Munch returned home, she had several messages on her answering machine. She paid her driver and sent him on his way before she played back the recordings.

The first and second calls were from Ellen. Humberto had called her and wanted to see Munch. Ellen didn't want to give him Munch's number, but couldn't think of a good reason not to, so she gave him a wrong number and was now screening her calls so she didn't have to talk to him again before Munch called back with instructions. The machine cut her off.

Ellen's second message was that she hoped Munch was doing okay, and was thinking of her, and hoped Munch didn't think she had forgotten where Munch was and what she was doing. Munch smiled. Some people didn't know what to say at times like these and others didn't know when to shut up.

The third call was from Roger. Her heart sped up at the sound of his voice.

"Call me when you get this," he said. "I'll be waiting."

He left a number. She dialed it.

"Munch?" he asked.

"Doesn't sound like you were expecting anyone but me."

"We have an opportunity to wrap this case up. Are you with me?"

"I guess that depends. What's in it for me?"

"You mean like your reward? I'm sure we can work out a commission."

"That's only part of it." A few days ago, the danger hadn't bothered her. She'd had blood in her eyes then, but now she was thinking more clearly.

"The sooner we shut down this ring," Roger said, his tone patient as if he were speaking to a small child, "the sooner we can unseal the indictments and reveal Rico's role in all this. That's what you want, right?"

"What do *we* have to do?"

"I need you to help me buy some dope," he said.

"What kind of dope?" she asked.

"Does it make a difference?"

"To some of us. Yeah. It does." She was pretty certain she could resist coke or pot, but much less sure that her sobriety was up to the ultimate test of her drug of choice. Heroin.

"Cocaine. You'd be wearing the wire."

"What weight?" she asked.

"A kilo to start."

She whistled. That was some serious money. The largest deal she'd ever been a part of was a half of an ounce. She didn't like the fact that she'd be so far out of her element. "I can't do any, you know, to like test it." Rico wouldn't want her sacrificing her sobriety, not that she would for him anyhow. "And I want an agreement in writing from you guys, saying I'm doing this for you."

Roger chuckled into the phone. "Don't you trust me? I'm crushed."

"I'm sure you're not. When do you want to do this thing?"

"As soon as you can set it up," he said. "You remember that big guy, Humberto? You met him at the house on Hampton?"

"Yeah, I know who you mean."

"He's the man I want to meet."

Munch chuckled now. "Yeah, *the man* is goddamn everywhere lately."

"Put out some feelers," Roger said. "Let it be known you're looking for him."

"I can do better than that. My best friend is helping with this case. She gave Humberto her number." Munch decided it was time to dispense with at least some of the bullshit. "But I'm not telling you anything you don't know already, am I? You get me the authorization for this deal in writing. Put down that Ellen Summers is a cooperating witness who I recruited to help us."

"All right."

"How long will all that take?"

"I'll be at your door in forty minutes."

Munch felt a little sick to her stomach. This was all moving too fast and seemed too easy. She should have asked for more time.

She called Fernando's house and asked to speak to Asia. "I'm going to be another hour at least, honey. Is that okay?"

"There's a boy named Sean here. He knows magic tricks."

"Is he any good?" Munch asked.

"Sometimes. He needs more practice."

"So you're okay for now?"

"Yeah, it's weird."

"What's weird?"

"I'm kinda having fun. Do you think that's okay?"

"Of course it is. I'll be there as soon as I can." She called Ellen next and spoke to her machine until Ellen picked up.

"The cops want me to help set up Humberto."

"How do you feel about that?" Ellen asked.

"Not great, but the sooner they close the case, the sooner they can release the truth about Rico."

"And you're sure that's what you want?"

"I've come this far, might as well see it through." Munch felt that uncomfortable tingling feeling again. Was she rushing into this? Or, more precisely, being rushed into it? "Next time he calls, give him my number. I'll be home."

"How much blow are we talking about?" Ellen asked.

"Pretty serious weight. A key."

"And what's to stop him from gunning for you after? Going to jail doesn't stop these guys. Some of those Mexican Mafia guys have more power in than out."

"So what are you saying? Because they're scary, we let them do what they want?"

"I'm just saying it isn't smart to be too obvious."

After Munch hung up, she laughed out loud. Ellen had just lectured her about being too obvious. Wasn't that one of the seven signs of the Apocalypse? It was definitely time to take the initiative, and that meant calling for reinforcements. She strode across the street and knocked on her biker neighbor's door.

From previous encounters, she knew the guy's name was Li'l Joe. In a reverse twist on the biker naming game, Joe really was little, for a guy, although he still had six inches on Munch. He was wiry and wore his dark hair in a ponytail. His beard was trimmed into a goatee, and like many small men, he was even-featured and handsome, the kind of guy she might have gone for back in the day. Not that that would happen now. Even if she weren't grieving, she was smart enough not to date a neighbor. Again, anyway.

"So I got the word about you," Joe said.

"Yeah, what was that?" Munch asked.

"You're under the protection of the Pride. Petey called and said I should look out for you."

"Yeah, me and Petey go way back," Munch said.

Li'l Joe arched his back as they spoke. Munch supposed she was meant to admire his physique, but what she was interested in was his untapped telephone.

She gave him a five-dollar bill. "I need to call a friend of mine in Sacramento. Can I use your phone?"

He took the cash and pointed to his kitchen. "It's in there."

"Thanks." She had to pass through the front room. The house was dark, the windows shuttered. It smelled like a brewery. Foldouts from *Easy Rider* magazines were stapled to the wood paneling. The glossy pictures featured custom scooters with lots of chrome and large-breasted white women draped across the seats. She wondered if he had the April 1977 issue, the one with her short story in it.

She decided that could wait for another time as she turned on the kitchen light, opened her address book and dialed Roxanne's work number.

"Department of Motor Vehicles, Records," a voice answered.

Munch asked for Roxanne Glantz. Roxanne had been a running partner in the bad old days. Munch and she had crossed paths when Munch was six months sober. Roxanne and another friend, Deb, were sharing a small house in Oregon then, drinking, snorting speed, and carousing with a motley biker club called the Gypsy Jokers. Munch's sobriety had so impressed Roxanne that when Munch's business in Oregon was over, Roxanne returned to Los Angeles and got sober herself. She had since gone back to school, learned about computers, and moved to Sacramento, where she got a lucrative job with the DMV, implementing new software.

"This is Roxanne," a familiar voice said.

"Hi, it's Munch."

"Hi yourself. What's new?"

Munch told her about Rico's death and the narcs putting a squeeze on her.

"What can I do to help?" Roxanne asked.

"I was hoping you'd say that. If I gave you a car's VIN number, could you find the previous owners?" The seventeen-digit VIN, or vehicle identification number, unlike a license-plate number, never changed and was found on the vehicle's registration and owner's certificate as well as on the car or truck's doorjamb, dashboard, and frame.

"Is it a stolen car?"

"In a manner of speaking. But I don't think it's hot."

"Yeah, I could do that, but let's keep it to ourselves."

"That was the very next thing I was going to ask."

Munch told Roxanne she'd call her back with the numbers, and then placed a second call. Ellen's answering machine was still on.

"It's me again," Munch said.

Ellen picked up immediately.

"I need you to help me with something. How quick can you get here?"

"Fifteen minutes," Ellen said.

"Don't park out front," Munch said.

"You got it."

Fifteen minutes later, Ellen arrived. She was dressed for her clandestine mission in a short dark shag wig, black leather jacket with matching pants, and aviator sunglasses. Very subtle. Munch told her what she needed and where to look, then gave Ellen a pad of paper and a pencil and had her wait out of sight for Roger's arrival.

CHAPTER TWENTY-THREE

ABEL DELAGUERRA CALLED FOR HIS MAN TO WASH AND fuel his black Suburban. *La Sombra* had convinced him that the trip across the border would be worth his while. Victoria entered the bedroom as he removed bundles of cash from the safe.

"Where are you going?" she asked.

He looked at his wife, wondering what it would feel like to have a partner. Someone with whom he could be completely free and open. Maybe there was something to all her books. "I am going to Los Angeles. I have some business there."

"Does Humberto want you to come?" she asked.

"No, he's doing something else for me. This is about something different."

Victoria waited. Abel knew she would ask no more questions. He used to tell himself it was for her own good, but that hardly made sense anymore. He owned the law and the local government. Who would give her trouble? These were excuses not to involve her in his life. No wonder she had become so distant to him.

"Some missing product of mine has shown up in Los Angeles. I am going there to buy information about that from a person I deal with from time to time." There was no reason to mention that this person was a woman. He didn't want to make Victoria jealous. "This seller will only deal with me. I should be back late tomorrow." He leaned over and kissed her mouth, which was open in shock. He had never taken the time to explain himself before. "This is the first day," he said, kissing her once more, "of the rest of our marriage."

Abel felt very brave as he climbed into the passenger side of his bulletproof truck.

"Vamanos!" he told the driver. They headed north. They would spend the night in San Diego, and then go see *La Sombra* the following day.

Abel had both fond and sad memories of Los Angeles. In his younger days, he had owned several promising fighters and made the trip to the States several times a month. He had reconnected with Enrique Chacón then. Enrique was doing some boxing himself, hoping to manage one day. He was already a cop, a patrolman, but with enough clout and initiative to make Abel's driver's speeding tickets disappear.

Abel had returned the favor with ringside seats at the next middleweight bout.

The years had forged a mutually beneficial relationship. Enrique had made a choice and picked a side. As his career progressed, so did his usefulness. Unfortunately, there were some warrants that Enrique could not make go away, and Abel had been advised that he should avoid personal appearances in the United States. This made him sad. Abel missed the cities of the North; his children had enjoyed the amusement parks; Abel missed Los Angeles for the boxing matches, race tracks, and live theater performances. He would like to go people-watching in Palm Springs again, a city famous for its celebrities and their flashy young wives. Victoria also missed all these things, plus the shopping at the fancy boutiques and department stores. She unfairly held Abel to blame. As if he were supposed to have control over the DEA.

These feelings of regret and loss brought Abel's thoughts full circle and back to Enrique. There had been rumors and accusations concerning Chacón's true loyalties, but those were most likely the backlash of jealousy. Successful men made enemies in this world.

Rico Chacón, God rest his soul, was a good man. He had proved himself. Abel had never wanted to believe otherwise. Besides, Rico had too much family on both sides of the border to risk a double cross.

Ellen waited for the arrival of the silvery-blue Shelby Mustang. Munch told her to hold off until the narc, Roger, was in the house for five minutes, and that if Ellen saw a white van or any van on the street, to forget the whole thing. Some other narc could be in it and watching, and Munch didn't want Ellen to get in trouble.

Ellen was really digging this undercover shit, even if the lines were getting blurrier all the time between who were the good guys and the bad. She didn't argue the point with Munch, but she really didn't want to set Humberto up for a fall. He wasn't a bad guy. Just this morning, he had sent her flowers. Pretty classy. She didn't see the cops sending any bouquets.

When this was over, Ellen thought she might look into getting a private investigator's license. Shouldn't be a problem, unless her moral turpitude conviction got in the way. She'd have to look up the wording of the exceptions. She knew she couldn't work for the city, but if her past convictions weren't related to the work she hoped to pursue, there were ways to get around the bonding thing.

The Shelby pulled up in front of Munch's house and Ellen studied the long-haired undercover agent who emerged. She wondered if she would have spotted him as a narc if she hadn't known. Maybe not, she had to admit. He didn't have that military bearing so many cops had trouble shedding. She knew she didn't like him. He'd already proved he was dishonest, trying to trick Munch with that phony on/off switch. Taking advantage of her was what he was doing. Munch was going through a vulnerable time and doing her best to set the world right. She sure didn't need this so-called representative of the law jerking her around.

After Roger had been in the house for a good five minutes, and with no vans in sight, Ellen approached the Shelby as if she owned it. The VIN number was right where Munch had said it would be, on the driver's side of the dashboard, close to the windshield. Ellen copied the numbers and took a quick look for any other incriminating pieces of evidence. There was a leather jacket on the back seat, some empty coffee cups and fast food wrappers on the floor, but nothing else easily visible. She kept on walking.

Humberto called Abel to check in, but Victoria answered instead.

"I was hoping to speak with your husband," he said.

"He's not here. He's on his way to Los Angeles."

Humberto stood up straighter. "Why is he coming here?"

"He got a phone call from someone saying that some of his product had shown up where it shouldn't and he went to check it out."

"This person who called, was it a man or woman?"

"He didn't say."

"When did he leave?"

"An hour ago. He said he'd call me tomorrow, from Los Angeles."

"Did he mention me?"

"Only to say that you were doing something else for him."

"That doesn't give me much time," Humberto said, already watching the traffic passing by with a nervous eye, especially the black Suburbans with tinted windows.

"What are you going to do?" Victoria asked, her voice sounding tinny and far away and unmistakably nervous.

"That will depend on the *patrón,*" Humberto said. He hung up, returned to his motel room, and double-locked the door. Sitting on one bed, he spread newspaper on the other, and then, one at a time, disassembled, cleaned, reassembled, and loaded his guns. He was calmed by the repetitive action of working a soft cotton rag saturated with linseed oil across the various parts, coaxing them to shine under the fluorescent lighting.

He needed to sell the remaining cocaine as quickly as possible. Time was running out. That feeling had been with him since the buy meet with the *negros*. Someone had put together the skeleton logo and tracking number on one of the keys he'd already unloaded, known what it meant and how to contact Abel. There was still a chance that Humberto had not been identified as the source. The odds were he had. From there it was a small leap for Abel to realize who his betrayer was. And Humberto knew full well how he dealt with traitors and rivals.

Humberto packed his weapons, clothes, newly acquired cash, and the remaining cocaine. He needed to set up base somewhere safe, where no one knew to look for him, and regroup. He drove the rental car into the alley and parked next to his truck. Working quickly, he removed the door panels on the Chevy, carefully pried back the insulating plastic, and stuffed the window cavities with drugs and money. He patted the hood of his truck in fond farewell, hoping that he wouldn't have to abandon his vehicle forever.

Ten minutes later he was on the busy freeway, heading for downtown.

Munch made Roger go through the plan one more time.

"So who are you again?"

"I'm a guy you went to school with. I left the neighborhood and went up to Alaska to work on the pipeline. Now I'm back in town and looking for good investments." He had asked her for the transmitter and now was popping the case open.

"But if you made so much money up there, why do you need to deal coke?"

"You're not looking at this like a criminal," he said.

This was the closest he'd come to giving her a genuine compliment. "And you think this scenario is believable?"

"It covers you if I get made," he said. He removed two 9-volt batteries from the black plastic case and set them on her kitchen table. "This is a win-win with minimal risk on your part. Don't worry about the cover story. Everyone understands the temptations of easy money."

Munch understood the American dream. She wanted more for herself and Asia, but she had her limits on what she would do and whom she would crawl over to get what she wanted. At the end of the day, what you really had was how you felt. A million dollars in the bank didn't mean anything when your gut was crawling with regret or fear.

She poured more lemonade into his glass. "You do this a lot, don't you?"

Roger avoided eye contact. "You mean these kinds of operations?"

She glanced at the clock over the stove. He'd been there twelve minutes. She wondered if he was carrying the gun that had put all those holes in Rico's chest. "Do you ever get to like the people you meet? The dealers?"

He shrugged. "Some of them are very likable. But hey, I didn't ask these people to break the law." He removed two new batteries from their cellophane wrapper and popped them into the transmitter.

"How about if somebody just got caught up in circumstances, and you saw they had potential to be like . . . I don't know . . . a good citizen later?"

"You mean would I cut them a break?"

"Or at least put in a good word for them."

"That's not my end of things." He handed her back the transmitter.

She turned the device over in her hands. "How long is this good for?"

"About five hours. I'll put fresh batteries in before the meet." He looked her in the eye. "I need to know now. Can you pull this off?"

She figured she'd given Ellen plenty of time, plus she wanted to get back to Roxanne before she left for the day. She made eye contact right back at Roger. "Sure, we're the good guys, right? Nothing's more black and white than that." She popped off the back cover and unsnapped the batteries. "No point in wasting these."

Roger looked a little perturbed, but what could he say?

Munch walked Roger out, turned on the garden hose, and made like she was attending to her front yard. The Shelby turned the corner and Ellen appeared from behind the neighbors' low block wall. She had already called the Shelby's VIN number in to Roxanne, using a pay phone.

"It came back as 'Record not on file,' " Ellen said.

"How can that be?" Munch asked.

"She didn't know. She'd never seen that before."

Munch moved the hose to another rosebush. "It was worth a try. It would have been nice to have this guy's home address, but oh, well."

"Roxanne said she didn't work tomorrow, but she'd do whatever she could for you," Ellen said.

Munch nodded as she spoke. "I've been getting that a lot lately." She turned off the hose.

Ellen went with her across the street to Li'l Joe's house. He had several friends over. Munch and Ellen looked at each other before crossing the threshold. An unspoken agreement passed between them. Women were much safer traveling in pairs among three or more male bikers. The guys were the most dangerous when they packed up. The wise biker chick also knew not to accept any drinks she didn't watch poured from a sealed bottle, and then never to leave that drink unattended.

"Can I use the phone again?" Munch asked.

Li'l Joe puffed out his bantam-rooster chest, "Sure thing, ladies. You want something to drink?"

"Thank you, darling," Ellen, always the diplomat, said. "Maybe later."

Munch went into the kitchen and called Mace St. John. Wouldn't the bikers freak to know she was using their phone to call a cop?

"Hi," she told him, "it's me."

"Are you home?" he asked.

"Not exactly. I'm at a neighbor's. Too many people on the line at my house, if you know what I mean."

"What's going on?"

"These cops want me to help them. I'm not undercover or anything. I'm just supposed to introduce this narc named Roger to one of Rico's contacts."

"Where will that leave you?"

"Exactly what I asked." She told him about the cover story.

"They can't make the case without you?"

"This just ends it that much faster," she said, feeling weird to be defending these guys.

"Have they said Rico was clean?"

"I told you he was."

"Yeah, right."

Munch turned her back on a biker who had wandered in the kitchen for ice. "I would think the exact same thing if they were saying these things about you."

"You want my advice?" St. John's voice sounded tired.

"Actually, I have a question. If I ran the VIN and plates on an undercover car, how would it come back?"

"It would be registered to the department, or, if it were a deep undercover car, it would be registered to a PO box or some kind of mail drop."

"What if it came back, 'No record on file'?"

"Then it would be a fed car. Why?"

"This guy Roger. I ran his plates, but I thought he was with the LAPD."

"DEA is more likely."

Well, there was a big surprise; Roger had neglected to mention that. "You think I can trust these guys?"

"Like I said before, your best interests aren't their first priority."

"What do you think I should do?" she asked.

"Get out of it if you can. Tell them you had a change of heart. I mean that. I want you to listen to me."

"I always do," she said.

"What are your immediate plans?"

"I've got to go pick up Asia, then I'll call Roger back and tell him it's a no-go."

CHAPTER TWENTY-FOUR

***LA SOMBRA* CHOSE TO MEET AT A HOTEL IN SANTA MON-**ica that overlooked the water. Abel arrived for the meeting at ten on that Sunday morning. He heard church bells as they arrived at the hotel's circular driveway. Abel thought of his wife and children back home, attending mass. He told his driver to wait with the car and then took the elevator to her fourth-floor room.

La Sombra answered her door.

He was surprised at her appearance, wondering who had been foolish enough to blacken her eyes and split her lip. Whoever it was, if he or she was still breathing, had a short unpleasant future in store.

She had hot drinks waiting for them on a tray.

"Are you still indulging?" she asked, showing him that she had brought hot chocolate and a small shaker of red pepper.

"How kind of you to remember," he said.

He waited until she had poured and blended his drink before he began. "Do you have it here?"

She strode purposely across the room to the closet and returned with a shoe box. He took the envelope of cash from his inside jacket pocket and placed it beside him on the settee.

She removed the lid of the shoe box. The cocaine had been removed and repackaged. He didn't mind, he wasn't buying back his own product. He recognized his logo immediately.

"Do you mind?" he asked, reaching for the wrapper.

She made a graceful gesture with her hand. "Please."

He unfolded the end flap and saw the number written there. This was indeed part of his stolen shipment. A cold fury swept through him. "Where did you get this?"

"I bought it. He gave me too good a price. That's when I got suspicious."

"Did you know the man?"

"Very well."

Abel tried to picture a cool mountain stream, willed his face into a peaceful expression, and made his tone light, as if he were asking for a spoonful of sugar. "And, señorita, would you be so kind as to tell me this man's name?"

"Certainly, for all the good it will do you. The man is dead. He was killed last week by the police. I think you knew him. Rico, he was called. Enrique Chacón."

The cool mountain stream Abel had envisioned evaporated. So it was him. The man he had treated as a son, well, perhaps not a son, but certainly a favored nephew. How dare he! Abel needed to get in touch with Humberto. Chacón had left behind a daughter and father, several brothers, and hadn't Humberto mentioned something about a fiancée? She would pay for his betrayal as well. How dare he!

"Wait a minute," Abel said. "You and Enrique. Weren't you lovers?"

"Ancient history." Christina pointed to her face. "Who do you think was responsible for this?"

"Not Enrique." The marks were too fresh.

"No, not Enrique. These last few months he wouldn't give me the time of day. It was the little bitch he was going to marry. She attacked me for no reason."

"May I use your telephone?" Abel asked, his rage making his voice tremble.

"Certainly," Christina said as she slung her bag over her shoulder. "I need to go out. Please make yourself at home."

"I might have another piece of business for you."

She nodded. "I expected this. Rico had family everywhere."

"I assume you want to deal with the fiancée yourself?"

"I would almost do it for free."

"Before you kill her, make her tell you where the rest of my cocaine is."

Christina hesitated only a second. "Got you."

"When will you be back?"

"Two hours. Order room service if you like. The omelettes here are very good."

Christina left Abel for the house on Hampton. It was time to implement the second phase of her plan, and that meant getting hold of Humberto and telling him what she had and hadn't done for him.

CHAPTER TWENTY-FIVE

HUMBERTO'S COUSIN COULDN'T BE MORE GRACIOUS. HE accepted Humberto into his home and offered him his own bed. Humberto told Felix not to be ridiculous, the couch would be fine. Now, as he stretched his cramped muscles, he wished he hadn't been so quick to refuse. They should have shared the bed, as they had when they were boys.

They had talked long into the night.

Felix had been excited to hear that Delaguerra was in town.

"He will have a bodyguard, and he still commands an army of loyal men," Humberto cautioned.

"So what?" Felix said. "I will gun him down like a dog, without warning. God is my witness."

"God witnesses many things. That doesn't mean He's on our side."

"Delaguerra deserves to die," Felix insisted.

"No doubt," Humberto agreed. "At this point you could even argue self-defense. I'm just saying that we must be smart, and not react with hot blood. I still intend to have a future when this is over. You deserve one, too, *mi carnal*. It is what your father would have wanted." Humberto had a quick image of his Uncle Nestor, who had died so needlessly. Over what? One careless snip of a rosebush. When Humberto returned victoriously to the ranch, he would make Victoria light the match that burned those roses to the ground.

Now it was ten-thirty in the morning and Felix was still asleep.

Humberto padded quietly into the apartment's small kitchen and put the makings of coffee into Felix's percolator. He shut the door to muffle the noise and dialed Chicken's number.

The phone rang six times before Chicken answered.

"Where have you been, *esse?* I came by the motel last night, but you were gone."

"Change of plan." Humberto found a coffee cup in the cabinet above the sink. "What did you want?"

"Those guys you met the other day. They're putting a thing together."

"Good."

"Oh, yeah, and that Christina broad wanted to get with you. She said you should call her as soon as you could. She said it was life and death. She's staying at some hotel in Santa Monica. Wait a minute, I'll get the number for you."

Humberto heard papers rustling, dogs barking and a string of curses. Christina. Of course. She would be the one. She had been to the Delaguerra ranch with Enrique. He'd kill the bitch with his own bare hands.

Chicken came back on the line with Christina's room and phone number. Humberto was repeating it back to him when Chicken interrupted. "Never mind, she just pulled up to the house. I've got to put the dogs out back, then I'll get her on the line."

Humberto listened to a string of more curses in Spanish and English and wondered what good those dogs did Chicken if he couldn't get them to obey his commands. Someday they'd turn on him and leave nothing but his bones.

Christina's voice cut into his thoughts. "Humberto?"

"What do you want?"

"You should be happy to hear from me."

"Oh, yeah?"

"I'm your new best friend."

"How's that?" he asked, not liking the confidence in her tone.

"I've just come from a very interesting meeting with a mutual friend. He was very concerned about some things he thought were his showing up where he didn't expect them."

"And what did you tell him?"

"It's what I didn't tell him that you should be interested in. The Americans have an expression I've always liked. They say: 'Possession is nine tenths of the law.' "

"What did the señor think of this expression?" Humberto asked.

She laughed. "Oh, I don't think that would have pleased him. I don't like telling people things they don't want to hear. That can be dangerous in our business."

"How are you going to please me?"

"In many ways. First, I'm going to make your life easier by buying the rest of your stock. Of course, you will give me a very good price since I am buying in bulk. Second, you will be pleased to know that you can go back home. Señor has some urgent work for you. He has been told the sad truth about Rico. Stealing from him and all. He wants to take stock, both here and back in Mexico."

"If you're lying to me—"

"How would I profit from that?"

Humberto had to concede that she made a good point. He wondered how good a deal he would have to give her. Then he looked toward the bedroom door of his sleeping cousin. If Abel Delaguerra was taken out, then Humberto wouldn't have to cut anyone a deal.

"Where is the señor now?"

"In my hotel room. Do you have the number?"

"Chicken gave it to me."

"Call there in an hour, after you've given this some thought."

Humberto poured himself a cup of coffee. He would indeed give the whole situation some serious thought.

Ten minutes later, he made a second call. Ellen answered, sounding wide awake.

"The flowers were beautiful," she said. "Thank you."

"It was nothing. I'm glad you liked them. I tried to call your friend Munch, but when I called the number I had for her, I just got all these strange beeps and whirs."

"Sounds like you got a fax machine." Ellen recited the number again.

"That's not the number I had," Humberto said. "The last two numbers were switched. Do you think she's home now?"

"I don't know. Probably. Why?"

"Something has come up. Can I come over and tell you about it?"

"Sure thing, darlin'. I've been missing you since you left."

Humberto smiled, happy to know his feelings were reciprocated. "I'll be there as soon as I can. Call Munch and tell her to meet us there. She might not be safe at home."

"Safe from who?"

"Just tell her to be careful."

Humberto hung up just as Felix stumbled into the kitchen. "Who was that?"

"A woman I know. I'll probably stay with her tonight."

He told his cousin about his previous conversation with Christina.

Felix listened intently. "Delaguerra is at this hotel now? Give me one of your guns."

"He won't be alone or unguarded. He wants to meet with me, probably to tell me to deal with Rico's family, as I was supposed to deal with you."

Felix shook his head. "He's a monster."

Humberto shrugged. Felix had lived in the States too long. He'd forgotten how the world worked back home. "He has gotten carried away."

"And soon they'll be carrying him away."

"I'm good with that, believe me, but let's find a way that doesn't get us killed."

Roger had not been pleased with Munch's change of heart. He promised to go back to his commander and see what he could do to sweeten the pot.

"This isn't about money," she told him.

"Did I say it was?" he replied.

He called her back twenty minutes later with an irresistible offer. Munch agreed to the new terms and then called St. John back.

"I told Roger I'd changed my mind and he came back with this: He said they'd make a formal announcement clearing Rico's name as soon as they make a buy from Humberto." She was proud of the deal, the way she'd prove all the doubters wrong.

"Before the case is fully adjudicated?" St. John asked, not sounding as thrilled as she would have liked.

"That's what he said."

"Something doesn't add up."

"I already said I would do it." She felt annoyed and let it show in her tone. Why couldn't he just be happy for her? Hadn't she had enough rain on her parade already?

"Just be very, very careful."

She had assured him she would. Then she had left for some much-needed one-on-one time with her daughter.

Consequently, she was not home to receive Ellen's worried call. She had taken Asia and Jasper to Mandeville Canyon. There were trails there too narrow for horses where Munch could let Jasper off his leash to explore. She brought water and a bowl so Jasper would have plenty of ammunition.

Asia made a game of counting how many times he lifted his leg to leave his mark.

"I'm going back to work tomorrow," she told Asia. "We need to get back into our routine."

Asia scratched her arm, but didn't say anything. Munch didn't know what she had expected and wondered if she put too much of a burden on the young girl's shoulders. Caroline St. John told her not to worry about that, that kids had a way of letting things they weren't ready to hear go over their heads. Munch hoped she was right about that.

Jasper trotted on ahead and Asia chased after him calling his name. It was a game they played. Asia pretended that Jasper was trained, Jasper pretended he was deaf.

She watched them romp in the dappled sunlight and tried to summon some pleasure from the scene. It was almost impossible to believe that a week ago her life had been completely different. How were either of them ever supposed to feel secure again? What was the point of making plans when so little of life was predictable? Maybe that wasn't fair; a great deal of life was predictable. It was that ten percent of unexpected shit that could make or break you.

But hadn't things that seemed terrible at the time turned out for the best? Going to jail, getting beaten up, raped, and robbed had all led to her eventual sobriety. Asia had come to her because her father was killed. Jobs, friends, apartments, even lovers had been ripped from her hands, only to be replaced by better ones.

One day, she would be able to get through an hour without crying.

One of these nights, she would sleep all the way through until morning.

The pain would lessen.

She was banking on it.

Munch took stock of her small brood. Asia's shoes were untied. A pigtail had come unbraided, and her pants were muddy. Jasper had managed to get a six-inch twig of sagebrush entangled in one of his ears and was dragging it along. They were both bright-eyed and panting. Was there a future reflected in those bright eyes, or was now the only time that was important?

"Okay, guys," she said, "let's turn back."

"Awwh," Asia said, "but we just got here."

"We'll come back next week if you want, but I have things I need to do."

Asia looked as if she wanted to argue the point, but then gave in. "Jasper," she shouted, "heel."

Jasper dropped to the ground and worked at something in his paw.

"C'mon, honey," Munch said to her daughter, "we'll head this way and he'll get the idea. We'll stop by Fernando's house and pick up your dress shoes." After the funeral, Asia had changed into more comfortable clothes. They didn't discover until they arrived home last night that she had left her shiny black patent leather shoes behind.

"At Grandpa's, you mean," Asia said.

"What?"

"He said I should call him Grandpa."

When they pulled up to the house in Lawndale, Fernando was nowhere in sight. The garage door was open and the radio was playing. There were two coffee mugs on the table, but the coffee had grown cold.

Munch picked up the cups and headed for the door leading to the kitchen. The night before, when she had picked up Asia, the house had been bustling with people. Rico's many brothers and cousins had been standing around the fire pit telling stories and laughing. Someone had given Cruz a beer and he was flushed and grinning. Fernando sat at the kitchen table, arguing with his wife's sister about something that had happened thirty-five years ago. The rest of the women bustled about, picking up plates and wrapping leftovers. Munch had found Asia in the middle of a group of kids her age, impatient for her turn on the rope swing, and telling them all in a voice that sounded eerily like Munch's own: "C'mon already. What are you waiting for? Christmas?"

So where was everybody now?

"Hello?" Munch called out.

"Grandpa," Asia echoed, "it's us."

Jasper ran ahead, sniffing the ground importantly.

Munch dumped out the cold coffee in the sink. A frying pan was on the stove, full of congealed scrambled eggs. Toast, already browned, peeked out from the top of the toaster. Munch opened the slider to the back.

All she found were footprints in the dirt and the silence of a graveyard.

"Maybe they're walking the dog," Munch said. She tried to sound unconcerned, but too many things about the condition of the house felt wrong.

She grabbed Asia's hand and began a systematic check of the other rooms. The bedrooms, bathrooms, even the closets. Everyone was gone.

"Uncle Cruz?" Asia yelled.

"Maybe he wandered off," Munch said. "And Fernan—your grandpa, took the dog to go look for him." She spotted Asia's shoes by the front door. As she picked them up, she noticed the front door was unlocked and unbolted. The doors to outside were always kept locked to prevent Cruz from leaving the house unattended. In all the activity yesterday, this had probably been overlooked. That didn't explain the two mugs of coffee in the garage. Or why the garage door had been left open. And wouldn't it have made more sense for Fernando to go looking for his son in his pickup truck? The pickup truck was still parked at the curb.

Munch took Asia with her into the kitchen. Sylvia's number was in the book by the phone; Munch dialed it. There was no answer, the machine didn't even pick up. Munch tried not to read too much into that. Maybe they had unplugged the phone or forgotten to turn the machine on.

Maybe there were too many maybes.

"Asia, did anyone say anything yesterday about all of them going to church today?"

Asia thought a moment. “No. Where is everybody?”

“I don’t know, honey, but I’m sure there’s a good explanation.” She didn’t say they would like that explanation. She had a terrible feeling she wouldn’t.

CHAPTER TWENTY-SIX

ST. JOHN WAS ON HOSE PATROL. CAROLINE HAD ASKED him to wash down the patio, and while he was at it, he shot everything in sight. The shrubs by the back door were dusty. The eaves of the small Craftsman-style house (a stone's throw from one of the Venice canals) hosted a colony of spiders. He noticed a bird's nest in the corner where the ceiling beams crisscrossed, but left it alone.

He placed unshelled peanuts on the top of the block wall surrounding his yard for the blue jays and refilled the feeder with seed for the smaller birds. Next he pulled an old comforter from the dryer in the garage and spread it on the concrete patio. Samantha, his elderly black Lab, stretched her arthritic limbs and lowered herself cautiously on the blanket.

St. John stroked her back gently and planted a kiss on her age-whitened muzzle. What more could one ask for in one's old age, he thought, but a spot in the sun, surrounded by loved ones? Brownie followed him faithfully, growling and tossing her head, trying to entice him into a game of catch.

His thoughts kept returning to Munch. Poor kid. And Rico, who was not such a bad guy, really. Despite the rumors. God knew, Munch had loved him.

He patted Brownie's head. "We'll play later."

St. John went into the kitchen, where Caroline was emptying the dishwasher. He watched her for a moment, enjoying the curves of hips and breasts twisting under her housedress. Maybe they'd play later, too.

He picked up the telephone.

"Who are you calling?" Caroline asked.

"Rumpelstiltskin." Their pet name for the medical examiner.

Caroline didn't miss a beat. "About Rico?"

"Yeah, Shue likes to catch up on his paperwork on Sunday mornings. He'll talk to me."

"Give him my love," Caroline said.

Mace smiled into the phone as it rang. Frank Shue was a character. Not the kind of guy you had over for dinner, especially if you were entertaining other guests. Many defenders had made the mistake of underestimating the man. Shue, even at the beginning of his workday, always appeared as if he had been spin-dried and then forgotten in the dryer. Caroline said he looked like an unmade bed with his shirt flaps always half untucked, tie askew, and flyaway hair. But the guy could make a corpse talk, even if he had the charisma of a chalkboard.

"Office of the coroner."

"It's St. John."

"What can I do for you?"

"Who did the post on Enrique Chacón?" St. John asked.

"Sugarman. In the aquarium. I assisted." The aquarium was the glass-walled room reserved for high-profile deaths, police officers, or suspects who had died in custody. As well as accommodating multiple observers, the autopsies performed there were also videotaped.

St. John was not surprised that Sugarman had handled the postmortem examination personally. He was the senior forensic pathologist and not afraid of controversy.

"Anything unusual?"

"I just got the tox results."

"And?" St. John asked.

"Clean. No narcotics or drugs of any kind."

“How about the bullet wounds?”

“The hits to his chest were consistent with LAPD ordinance.”

“What about the head wound?” St. John asked.

“The head wound?”

St. John could hear the man scrambling for time. “Rico’s fiancée saw the body before the mortuary cleaned it up.”

“How unfortunate.”

“She said the shot looked like it had come from close range. The hair was singed around the entry wound.”

“We’re not publishing any details about that.”

“What does that mean?”

“I’m not at liberty to say.”

St. John didn’t press, not wanting to put Shue or Sugarman in an awkward position. If he was inferring correctly, the head wound, most likely the kill shot, had not come from a police weapon. Who would benefit from keeping that information quiet? If the guy was dirty, shooting at his own, then no one was going to suffer any consequences for shooting him.

If he was clean, as Munch believed and as this Roger guy claimed to back up, then why was he shot, and by whom? And why keep that information secret in the first place?

Caroline walked into the kitchen with a leash in her hand. She took one look at her husband, who was staring at a spot on the wall, and didn’t say a word. She knew he was working. He heard the door shut behind her as she left to take Brownie for a walk.

If Rico was shot by the bad guys, yet not a bad guy himself, and the department was keeping it quiet, there were several possible explanations. Perhaps they were protecting an ongoing investigation. If Rico was only pretending to be on the take, perhaps the task force didn’t want the bad guys aware that Rico had been playing for the good guys all along and that supply routes and connections were compromised.

Okay, that all worked.

Then the logic went screwy.

Why was the DEA guy helping Munch prove that Rico was clean before the case was finished? It wasn't to help Munch, that was for damn sure. They had their own agenda. Maybe they still had an asset or implanted agent. Revealing that Rico was himself a double agent might protect their operative still in play. But if that was true, would revealing the truth now put Munch in unnecessary jeopardy? Was giving Rico a commendation at this point worth the wrath of the narcotraffickers? And why the change of strategy?

Something must have happened to cause a script change. And knowing how some of these narcs operated, Munch was probably an expendable asset as far as they were concerned. It was time to let them all know she had friends.

Humberto needed his own army, and for that he needed cash. He left Ellen to wait for Munch's return call and told Chicken to meet him in Compton. The black guys Chicken hooked him up with had put together enough cash to buy five more kilos.

He would save three or four for Christina, and tell her he had already sold the rest. How could she possibly know different?

He dropped Chicken off back at the house on Hampton and drove alone to the apartment where he had conducted his business with the duplicitous Christina. When he went back to her apartment, there was a FOR RENT sign in the window and her car was gone.

She must have taken up residence in the hotel, knowing she was safer there. He could do nothing to her or with her while she was in the company of Delaguerra. The time was not yet right to take the *Jefe* down.

"I'm going to go in for a while," Mace St. John told his wife when she returned from her walk.

"I had a feeling," she said.

He bent down and kissed her. His windbreaker swung open, revealing his gun and badge. "I'll call you if it's going to be more than a few hours."

"Good; I'm taking out steaks."

He smiled at the bribe. She only allowed him red meat once a week.

Twenty minutes later, St. John was at his desk on the second floor of the West Los Angeles Police Station looking in his oldest card carrier. St. John kept the cards of every cop he met and organized them in albums according to county, division, and branch of law enforcement. Art Becker's card was in the oldest card carrier he owned. The back cover was detaching from the spine and the corners were rounded from constant handling.

The cards inside belonged to cops who had at some time worked in the Pacific Division. When Mace had been there, it had been called the Venice Police Station, but that was a million years ago. Art Becker was one of the few dinosaurs who had never left. He'd also been Rico's first partner in Los Angeles.

St. John slipped the card from the plastic insert and called the number written on the back. Becker's unlisted home phone rang twice. The men exchanged brief amenities.

"How you holding up?" St. John asked.

"It hurts to lose one. You know that."

"Can I buy you a beer?"

"Is it important?" Becker asked.

"Yeah, it really is. You know Chapman in Narcotics?"

"Sure."

"Him, too."

Becker sighed. "Yeah, no problem. I've been expecting this call."

"Okay," St. John said, his curiosity totally piqued. He should have done this sooner.

"Chez Jays in twenty?"

St. John checked his watch. "You got it."

Chez Jays was a dive, but a landmark dive. The diminutive bar had a key location, across the street from the Santa Monica Pier and next door to the Rand Corporation, a federally funded think tank where intelligence on the Pacific Rim, the Middle East, Russia, and Eurasia was gathered, analyzed, and disseminated to the various defense agencies.

Sawdust covered the floor and signed movie posters adorned the walls. It was a bar made for serious drinking, international intrigues, and secret trysts. The only light allowed in was from the front door, certainly not the windows, which were few and small and painted over. New arrivals were temporarily blinded until their eyes adjusted to the dark, giving the embedded patrons that extra minute which might make the difference between a dressing-down and a divorce.

Becker was already there when St. John arrived, seated in one of the red Naugahyde booths and munching on a basket of french fries.

"Chapman should be here in about ten minutes. He has to drive up from El Segundo."

St. John eyed the french fries with longing, but didn't indulge. "How'd you get him to come?"

Becker's eyes were all but lost under puffy lids. "He feels just as bad as I do about all this."

"Fill me in," St. John said.

"Rico was working on a multi-agency task force, even the Mexicans were involved."

"You found two that weren't corrupt?" St. John asked.

Becker attempted a smile, but his eyes and the rest of his face weren't having it. "It's not so much a matter of who's corrupt or not, as who can be controlled."

The waitress brought Becker a beer. She turned to St. John, "What'll you have, hon?"

"7-Up."

Becker took a sip of beer and continued. "Anyhow, it's mostly a fed-run deal, but local law enforcement in San Diego, Los Angeles, Nogales, and Calexico are also involved. The feds know that the economies of the countries south of the border are too dependent and intertwined with the drug trade to expect an end to business anytime soon. So, they figured, shit, can't beat 'em, might as well get our foot in the door."

"You're telling me we've gone into business with these guys?" St. John was disgusted. He'd heard rumors about the funding of the Contras in Nicaragua. Between his tours in Nam and years on the job, he also knew how the CIA liked to play. Friendly dictators such as Noriega, the Shah of Iran, and Ferdinand Marcos were all backed by the U.S. of A. And who knew how many others had been nudged into power covertly?

"What they hoped to do was put kinder, gentler kingpins in power," Becker said. "Guys we could hold a hammer over, and later use to get to the bigger guys."

"So the guy might still be a son of a bitch, but he's our son of a bitch."

"That's about right."

"Sounds like a tough assignment. Any hombre with the balls and business sense to run a cartel isn't going to be easily manipulated."

The conversation paused while the waitress delivered St. John's soft drink. Someone upwind lit a cigarette and St. John felt a surge of desire. He knew Caroline would kill him before the nicotine had a chance if he came home with tobacco on his breath.

Becker leaned forward and spoke quietly. "I think the official/nonofficial term, if you know what I'm saying, is person of mutual sympathies."

"What's all of this got to do with Chacón?" St. John asked.

The front door swung open and the figure of a man made a black hole in the bright light.

"Chapman," Becker called. "Over here."

Chapman wound his way past the large wooden ship's wheel at the entrance and over to their table. Becker made the introductions and the men shook hands.

"I've heard of you," Chapman said. "You worked in Robbery/Homicide downtown, right?"

"Yeah, I'm in West LA now."

"How's that?"

"Quiet." St. John knocked on the wooden table, feeling the chill of cop superstition. Unspeakable evils usually befell a detective heard muttering, "Boy, it sure is quiet around here."

Becker and Chapman chuckled.

"I've been hearing about you, too," St. John said.

"Uh-oh," Chapman said, straining to sound jovial. He flagged down the waitress and ordered a Scotch.

"It's about Rico," Becker said.

Chapman's smile evaporated. "Friend of yours?"

"I'm closer to the woman he was going to marry. Munch Mancini. In fact, my wife and I are godparents to her daughter."

"She never said—"

St. John didn't let him finish. "She wouldn't. She's funny that way, doesn't ask for special treatment. I'd hate to see her getting dicked around."

"Tell him," Becker said. "Tell him everything. If you don't, I will."

CHAPTER TWENTY-SEVEN

MUNCH WENT HOME WITH ASIA IN CASE THERE WAS SOME news on her machine. The only message waiting for her was from Ellen. She had called around eleven. It was now a little past noon.

Munch was pretty sure the cops had her phone tapped, but she wouldn't bet her life on it. She retrieved Rico's gun from the highest shelf in her closet and the boxes of extra bullets. Six shots might not be enough, she thought, and filled her pockets with spare rounds.

She also grabbed the transmitter Roger had given her, popped the batteries back into place, and strapped the device around her waist; then she returned Ellen's call.

"I'm home now. What's up?"

"You should get out of there, come over here. Humberto doesn't think you're safe."

"Safe from whom?"

"He didn't say. Pretty nice of him to care, don't you think?"

Now Munch felt like shit. This was the guy she was supposed to bust or at least set up to get busted. She couldn't be quite as cavalier as Roger was about all this. She almost envied Roger his moral certainty. She had never had an easy time of pigeonholing people as good or bad.

"What are you going to do?" Ellen asked.

"I'm going to lock the doors and take a bath. I'm feeling dirty."

Victoria was of two minds. As little as three months ago, she would have been overjoyed at Abel's efforts to communicate and work on their relationship. She believed in the institution of marriage, and she was not so cynical as to have lost all hope for romance rekindled.

Humberto was all right, but would never have Abel's fire. She was reasonably certain that only one of the two men would be returning from their trips north. Up until yesterday, she had prayed for widowhood with the caveat that Abel not suffer. But yesterday, she had glimpsed a different side of her husband. And a future that might still be possible.

But she had gone too far already, hadn't she? Even if somehow he survived, what if he were to discover the truth? How she had plotted against him. There would be no forgiveness for that. Although, if Humberto died quickly, who would tell on her?

And if Humberto returned, would he honor their pact or put her out into the street? That wouldn't do either. If Abel had taught her anything, it was to look after her own interests. With a heavy heart, she went into her children's rooms and gathered them to her. Roberto was the oldest at ten, followed by eight-year-old Ilda, and last, the youngest, already walking at eleven months, baby Carmelita.

"We're going on a little trip," she told them. "I want you each to bring your favorite toy."

"Is Daddy coming, too?" Roberto asked.

She looked down into her son's trusting eyes, ran her fingers through his curls, and said, "He's going to meet us there."

"Can I bring two toys?" Ilda asked. She batted long curling eyelashes, already a con artist plying her feminine wiles.

How could Victoria refuse her darlings anything? Wasn't it going to be hard enough, ripping them from the only home they'd ever known?

"All right. Two each, but hurry. And change out of your church clothes. We're going to have a picnic later. Bring your coats, too."

Victoria picked up the children's school packs, emptied them, and took them to her bedroom. She lifted the portrait of the Virgin from the wall above the dresser to reveal the combination safe. Abel hadn't cleaned it out yesterday, but he'd taken at least thirty thousand dollars. She grabbed the remaining bundles of hundred-dollar bills and stuffed them into the children's backpacks.

When that safe was empty, she went into the closet. Abel didn't know she knew about the second safe behind his shoe rack. He would be equally shocked that she had the combinations. She liked to think he would be impressed, maybe even a tiny bit proud at her resourcefulness.

The second safe yielded South African krugerrands, thousand-peso notes, a black velvet pouch of diamonds, and several handguns. She wrapped them carefully and hid them among her paints and brushes.

She had the cook pack a basket and had the driver, Adan, bring one of their Suburbans around. He also helped her load several canvases, her easel, and the wooden box of paint supplies into the back of the truck. She carried the children's backpacks herself, in case Adan commented about their weight, and slung them casually in the back seat, along with the baby's diaper bag.

While Adan filled the tank from the ranch's own pump, she returned to the villa for the children.

Carmelita was getting bigger every day, but she still fit nicely on Victoria's hip.

"Looks like we're going to make a day of it," Adan said.

"With children, you have to be prepared for anything," she said.

"I hope to find that out myself one day," he said.

She gave him another long look. "You're not married, are you?"

"No, señora. Not yet."

The villa was miles from the main road. They drove in silence down the long driveway. The children were absorbed in their private games, but Victoria stared out the window, committing the property to memory. She doubted she would ever see it again.

She noticed a glint of something coming from the mountains to the east. The sun, perhaps, playing on a metal gun barrel or the glass lenses of binoculars or a camera. It occurred to her that she was probably getting out at just the right time.

"Where to, señora?"

"South."

"So tell me what you know so far," Chapman said. He'd drained his Scotch in record time and snapped his fingers for the waitress to bring another one.

"I told him about the feds' plan," Becker said, answering for St. John.

The waitress returned with a cheeseburger for Becker and a second drink for Chapman. St. John was still nursing his soda and shook his head when the waitress pointed at it.

"Okay," Chapman said. "Chacón met this Mexican heavy named Abel Delaguerra when he was down in San Diego. Delaguerra was running some fighters back then. This was the late seventies. Chacón was still a kid and had aspirations of his own. Delaguerra's driver got a speeding ticket, and it wasn't his first. He was looking at losing his license and Delaguerra didn't want to have to replace him. He sees Chacón in uniform and asks him if there was anything he could do."

St. John nodded. Seemed about right. A peroxide blonde at the bar laughed loudly at something her escort said. St. John wondered if she was working.

"So Chacón goes to the courthouse the day the driver is there to contest the ticket," Chapman continued. "He sees the motorcycle cop who wrote the ticket and asks him if maybe he could develop a case of amnesia."

Becker picked up the story. "The motorcycle cop knows Rico from briefings and such and says, 'You know who that guy was driving for?' Rico's still thinking Delaguerra is a high-rolling fight manager. Course he never came out and asked 'cause, like Chapman said, he was looking to break into the game himself. Figured Delaguerra would be a good friend to have."

Becker took a bite of his burger and Chapman, his eyes slightly glassy, picked up the narrative. "The motorcycle cop tells Chacón that Delaguerra is a big-time pot smuggler and distributor."

"Rico had no idea," Becker added.

"Says he," Chapman said.

Becker's small eyes went cold and flat. "Yeah, that's right. Says he and I believed him."

Chapman raised his palms in surrender.

St. John could see both sides. Sure, Rico had been intentionally naive. But who hadn't? No matter what opinion he offered now, St. John would be betraying someone. "So then what happened?"

"Rico goes to his commander—" Becker said.

"Or his commander comes to him," Chapman interrupted.

"Whatever," Becker said. "You tell the story, all right?"

"Chacón was encouraged to keep a toe in the water." Chapman smirked. "But he's a young buck, right? So he does some creative interpretation to those orders and uses other body parts. Seems Delaguerra has this hot young wife. I mean young. She'd be jailbait here, but they do things differently down south.

"In the meanwhile, the Colombians come to Delaguerra. They've noticed how successful he is at moving product over the border and they make him an offer. Now instead of making a couple hundred profit on each key of pot, Delaguerra starts transporting cocaine. He's making five thousand a kilo, but he doesn't stop there.

"If he can make five grand for just moving the stuff, what if he gets into sales and distribution? He arranges for the Colombians to start paying him in product. On a thousand-kilo shipment, he gets fifty kilos in payment."

"One thousand kilos at a shot?" St. John asked, staggered at the amount.

Chapman sipped his drink. "I shit you not. We figure Colombia exports fifty tons a year, Peru three hundred tons, but that's Miami's problem."

"The upshot is that Rico gets in deeper and deeper," Becker said. "He wants out. The powers-that-be agree that it's gotten too dangerous. Rico introduces Delaguerra to new contacts and gets transferred to Los Angeles with a cover story that the department forced him into the move.

"Rico's happy, anything to distance himself from Delaguerra, who was getting wiggy. I'm talking dangerous wiggy. Taking out whole families of people who cross him. Not just spouses, but babies, cousins, grandparents, everyone. The law here can't touch Delaguerra because he won't cross the border, and he owns the law in Mexico."

"Why doesn't someone just take him out?" St. John asked. "Sounds like he's a waste of skin."

Chapman tipped the last of his drink into his mouth and started working on the ice cubes. "Suicide mission, for one thing. Guy has his own private army, lives on a ranch with only one road in and out. The perimeter is constantly patrolled by security guards with binoculars, walkie-talkies, and AK15s. When he does venture out, he travels in bulletproof Suburbans, driven by bodyguards. I mean this dude is totally paranoid."

"Yeah," Becker said, "nothing like surveilling a guy twenty-four hours a day to see that side of him."

"Can't throw down on him with a rocket without taking out a bunch of civilians, not to mention his wife and kids. According to Chacón, the wife is a virtual prisoner. She never goes anywhere without a watcher. Before Chacón cut ties with her and stopped going down to the ranch, he proposed a plan to smuggle her out."

"When was this?" St. John asked.

Chapman cracked some ice between his molars. "A couple, maybe three years ago. In '83 or '84."

So before he met Munch, St. John thought. "Your DEA buddy Roger told Munch that if she introduced him to some big guy named Humberto, the government would issue a formal statement exonerating Rico."

"She doesn't want that," Chapman said.

"Not while Delaguerra is still running things," Becker said.

"Who's this Humberto guy?" St. John asked, thinking he needed to get to Munch and warn her.

"Humberto Salcedo is the guy our government has tapped to succeed Delaguerra," Chapman said.

"When is this going to happen?" St. John asked.

"It's in the works," Chapman said.

"All right. Fine," St. John said. "But you still haven't told me who killed Rico Chacón and why?"

Chapman's beeper went off. He looked down at the display and said, "Uh-oh. I better see what this is about." He was on the pay phone for only a minute, and then came running back to the table.

CHAPTER TWENTY-EIGHT

MUNCH HAD ASIA TAKE THE FIRST BATH WHILE SHE FED Jasper.

She had filled the bathtub with hot soapy water for herself when she heard the front door open.

"Asia?" she yelled.

"What?" Asia yelled back.

"What are you doing?"

"We're going to play out front."

"Stay inside. You've been out enough today."

Asia didn't answer and Munch didn't hear the door shut again. Knowing Asia, she was propped in the open doorway, technically not "out."

Annoyed, Munch re-buttoned her shirt, but left it untucked. Almost as an afterthought she grabbed Rico's gun and pushed it into the waistband of her pants. When she checked the living room, the front door was open, but Asia was nowhere to be seen.

Annoyance turning to alarm, Munch crossed the room. Jasper was in the front yard, growling at a woman with long black hair who had Asia by the arm.

It was that bitch Christina. She had a hand around Asia's mouth and was dragging her toward the open back door of a van.

Munch sprinted across the front yard, Rico's service revolver now in her hand as she sneaked around the front of the van.

Asia must have bitten Christina's hand because Munch heard her sharp "Ouch," followed by Asia screaming, "Let go!"

Christina handed Asia to a cohort. Munch saw the hands reach for her little girl and she knew a cold fury. The time to act was now, while the kidnappers were distracted by their disobliging victim. Asia had been taught never to cooperate with her own abduction.

She yelled and kicked, "You're not my mommy. Let me go."

Christina said, "I'm not going to hurt you. I'll take you to your mommy."

Rico's gun was a standard-issue police revolver: a double-action .38. There was no safety. Pulling the trigger the first time cocked and fired the weapon. Munch had her finger wrapped around the trigger and needed little encouragement. She put the barrel of the gun to the back of Christina's head. "I'll save you the trouble."

"Wait," Christina said.

The second kidnapper was visible now. It was another woman. She was Anglo, with strong arms and short blond hair.

Munch addressed her, "Let go of my kid. Now!"

The woman complied.

"Asia, get out of the van."

Asia scrambled out of the van and stood behind her mother.

Munch was wearing the transmitter, but she had no idea if Roger was in range. "Put your hands up and away from your body."

The women did as they were told.

"We're DEA," Christina said.

"Bullshit."

"Rico and I worked together. That's all. We were co-workers. I wasn't doing him."

Munch almost laughed. "You think that matters to me now? Where were you taking Asia?"

"To safety. She's targeted. You're all targeted."

"So why didn't you come to me first?" Munch asked. "Or call me, some kind of warning? You're telling me you just snatch kids off the street, and that's standard operating procedure? You think I'm stupid?" Her finger tightened on the trigger. Squeeze it slowly, Rico had told her. Though at this range, aim and trajectory weren't going to be a problem. She wanted to push the barrel through the woman's skull.

"We're running out of time," Christina said.

Asia's hands clung to the back of Munch's shirt. "You are," said Munch.

"We've already moved the rest of the family," Christina said. "The father, the brothers, the ex-wife, Rico's daughter."

"You're telling me we're all targeted?" Munch was starting to see some logic in all this. She thought of the photographs she'd seen at Rico's house, seemingly taken when they were all unaware. She kept the barrel of the gun pressed to Christina's head. There could be many explanations of how and why Christina knew about all this.

"That's how these guys operate," Christina continued. "Someone betrays the cartel and the whole family gets taken out."

Munch felt a horrible realization blooming. "So all this time I've been trying to prove Rico was a good cop. . . ."

"You've been sentencing his whole family to death. Including you and your daughter. His daughter. Everyone."

"Did he know that? Did he understand that his job put us all at risk?" Munch still hadn't lowered the gun, but she'd eased off the trigger.

Tears streaked Christina's cheeks. "Of course he knew that. Why do you think he sacrificed himself?"

Munch kept working it through her brain, testing the logic out loud.

"I went to his dad's house. It was empty. And there was no answer at his ex-wife's house."

Christina nodded slowly. "That's right. They've all been taken somewhere safe."

"You got some ID? A badge?"

Christina looked nervously up the street. “No, I’m in deep undercover. I’m not carrying any of that.”

Munch gestured with her chin toward the blonde. “What about your partner here?”

“Sharon,” Christina said, “did you bring your ID?”

Munch noticed the blinds across the street in Li’l Joe’s house flick open. She also noticed a black Suburban with tinted windows turn the corner. Coming from the other end of the street was a Chevy Malibu, and behind that, a white van. The front door to Li’l Joe’s house opened. Joe and two other hungover bikers in full chains and leather stumbled into the sunshine.

“Everything all right?” Li’l Joe asked, squinting her way.

Munch noticed he kept his right hand behind his back. “I don’t know,” she called back. Then to Asia: “Get in the house. Take Jasper and get in your closet.”

Asia blanched.

“Do it now!”

The black Suburban slowed to a crawl. Munch tried to see the driver or if there were passengers, but the windows were too dark, even the windshield. A voice in her brain protested, *Hey, that’s illegal*. She turned back to look at Christina and the one she’d addressed as Sharon. Both women looked worried, almost panicked. Munch looked at the truck again and saw that the license plates were Mexican.

There was the sound of screeching tires and then a loud smack. The Suburban jolted forward, a horn went off behind it. Everyone looked at the two vehicles. Munch turned to see what the cars coming the other way were doing.

The blue Monte Carlo pulled halfway into the Okie’s driveway, blocking Christina’s van from making a quick exit. Humberto got out and jogged toward the Suburban. He had a gun in each hand.

Ellen emerged from behind the Suburban. A trickle of blood ran down her face from a cut on her cheek and she was yelling, "What are you, blind?"

She thumped the door of the Suburban, but the windows remained up.

She yelled over at the bikers, "Did you see this fool stop in the middle of the road?"

The white van had pulled to the curb. "Is that you, Roger?" Munch asked quietly into her microphone.

The headlights flashed on and off.

Munch was still holding Rico's gun on Christina. "There are two women here. I've met Christina before over at the Hampton house. Sharon is inside the van where you can't see her. They say they're DEA. Is that true? Flash once for yes."

The headlights flashed once.

"Give me the gun," Christina said.

Before Munch could decide whether that was what she wanted to do, a single shot went off behind her. A short bang, followed by a scream. Ellen.

Munch ducked and turned. Ellen lay in the street near the driver's door of the Suburban, which was now open. Blood spread across Ellen's sleeve, originating from some point above her left elbow. She gripped her shoulder, her face twisted with pain and fury. The driver, the shooter, was stepping out of the Suburban. The gun was still in his hand as if he intended to finish Ellen off.

Munch took cover behind a tree. She drew a bead and fired. Her shot went wide to the right. The tinted layer of glass on the back-door window splintered into a spider web of cracks, but didn't shatter. The driver ducked behind his open door. Ellen scrambled to the sidewalk and found another tree to hide behind.

Humberto was halfway between Christina's van and the Suburban. He dropped to the ground and rolled. At the first shots, Li'l Joe and his buddies produced their own guns and peppered the Surburban with small arm's fire. Two tires went flat. Munch threw her free arm over her head.

Christina reached under a quilted mover's blanket on the van's floor and pulled out an Uzi submachine gun. Using the back door of the van as cover, and standing on the rear bumper, she sprayed a burst at the bikers across the street. The shots went high creating an array of dark holes in the stucco. Whether that had been her intention, Munch couldn't tell.

Li'l Joe and his cohorts dived for cover inside his house.

In all that, Munch lost sight of Humberto. Roger never came out of the van. Munch expected to hear sirens, bullhorns, maybe a helicopter or two. But a minute or two had passed since the shooting began, and it didn't look like the cavalry was going to arrive in time.

Munch wanted to get to Asia. Just as many people died from ricochets and strays as the victims who were the intended targets. But getting to Asia would involve running up the sidewalk to her gate or vaulting over the four foot chain-link fence surrounding her front yard and then making a run for the front door. Both attempts would leave her open and vulnerable. Ellen's tree was closer to the gate. Besides, her blood was now dripping to the ground. She needed to dress her wound.

"Ellen," Munch called in a low urgent whisper.

Ellen looked over. "What?"

"You okay?"

"Hell, no. I've been shot."

"Go for the house," Munch said. "I'll cover you."

Ellen glanced behind her. "Let's both go," she said.

"No, your chances are better. I need you to make sure Asia's okay."

Ellen looked at the gate, then back at the van where Christina had her machine gun pointed out toward the street. "What's she doing here?"

Munch lifted her shirt to show Ellen that she was wearing the transmitter. "She's a friend of Roger's."

Ellen's eyes grew big. Munch felt something hard press against her ribs.

"Who's Roger?" Humberto asked as he took the gun from her hand. He peeled back her collar and saw the microphone looped through her bra strap. "What have you done?" he asked.

CHAPTER TWENTY-NINE

ST. JOHN GRABBED CHAPMAN'S ARM, DETERMINED NOT to let him go until he got some answers. "What's up?"

"Something's going down at your girlfriend's house," Chapman said. "It looks bad."

St. John threw a five on the table and ran for his car. Becker followed, breathing hard. "Let's take mine. I'm in a cruiser."

"You carrying a gauge?" St. John asked.

"The works," Becker said.

St. John quickly agreed. A shotgun might come in handy.

Becker got behind the wheel, while St. John affixed the magnetic beacon to the roof of the sedan. St. John listened for Munch's address on the radio chatter, and gripped the handholds on the dash and above his door as Becker threaded through the Sunday-noon beach traffic, code two.

Roger watched the scene unfold through his windshield. He was observing the whole operation collapse into chaos and there was nothing he could do about it. He cursed in frustration as he tore off his headset. Munch's wire had stopped transmitting. He couldn't see from his angle if she was inside Agent Christina Garcia's van or not.

The local cops' dispatchers had been advised not to respond to the shots fired. He was monitoring the police band and so far that end of the plan was holding up. Broadcasting over police frequencies would bring every goddamn reporter and thrill-seeking yahoo with access to a scanner. There were already way too many civilians involved.

Humberto Salcedo and Abel Delaguerra having their inevitable confrontation here and now was definitely not what they had wanted to happen. Heads were going to roll on this one. He'd be writing reports until Christmas.

The Suburban pulled forward until it was alongside Garcia's van and blocked his view of the scene even more.

His only consolation was that Garcia hadn't hit her panic button, so she must believe that the situation was still salvageable, not to mention her cover.

Roger didn't know where Humberto Salcedo was either. The guy moved surprisingly fast for such a big man. Roger had seen him cross in front of Garcia's van, then he'd lost him when he got to the sidewalk.

What were they doing?

A loud buzz sounded and Roger jumped. Garcia had hit her panic button.

Munch felt the transmitter heating up at the small of her back. The antenna wire must have popped loose, which meant that Roger wasn't getting any of this.

The Suburban pulled forward until it was between Christina and Li'l Joe's house. Christina lifted the barrel of her Uzi from the doorjamb.

The Suburban's driver and passenger, to avoid being vulnerable to the armed bikers, emerged from the driver's side with guns drawn. Now Christina was surrounded by dangerous and unpredictable drug dealers. To her credit, she was completely cool.

"Señor Delaguerra," she said. "What are you doing here?"

Delaguerra pointed at Munch with his pistol. "Is this the one?"

"She says she doesn't know anything about your product,"

Christina said, giving Humberto a meaningful look that Delaguerra could not see.

"And you believe her?" Delaguerra asked.

"I plan to discuss it further."

Munch still felt Humberto's gun in her back. The transmitter was burning her now, but to draw attention to it was certain suicide.

Delaguerra looked at Humberto. "And is questioning one small woman a job that requires both of you?" he asked suspiciously.

Munch prayed that the earth would open, swallow Delaguerra, and take him straight to hell. She didn't even care if they all had to die together, as long as she got to see Delaguerra go down. She wondered what the deal was with Humberto. He had to know Christina was a cop now, yet he wasn't dropping the dime on her. Ellen and Munch had speculated that Humberto and Delaguerra's wife had something on the side. Was this what Christina had on Humberto?

The reference to missing product meant someone must have ripped Delaguerra off, and Delaguerra obviously believed that Munch had something to do with that. This could only mean that Rico had been implicated.

Who would have pointed the finger at Rico? Either the real thief or someone who wanted leverage on the real thief.

A woman groaned inside the van.

"Who's this?" Delaguerra asked. He beat a hand on the side of the van. "Come out of there."

He said something in Spanish to his driver and the guy went over to the passenger door of the van. A moment later, Sharon stumbled out and was herded over to join the group. Her eyes weren't tracking right, and her short blond hair was matted with blood. One of those stray bullets must have caught her.

Sharon sank to the ground. Christina glanced at her fellow agent and shrugged. "I've got a doctor who will see her."

Munch had to hand it to her, Christina had some kind of nerve. Munch hoped she was also quick on her feet.

Make them protect you, Rico had written in his last note to her.

"I don't know what this bitch told you," Munch said, pointing at Christina, "but whatever it was was a lie. She's just jealous."

"What's this?" Delaguerra asked in an amused tone. "The little tiger roars?"

Humberto dug his gun a little sharper into Munch's back. Christina swung the barrel of her Uzi so that it was level with Munch's chest.

"Hey," Humberto said. "Watch it."

"So now you want me quiet?" Munch said. "Which is it? You know the truth. He didn't want you. He was marrying me."

"He loved me, you little whore," Christina screamed as she charged. The men stepped back as Christina and Munch went down together on the pavement, but instead of the cat fight they were expecting, Christina swung the Uzi around so that it was trained on Delaguerra and his man.

Delaguerra aimed and Christina fired. Small tufts of smoke wisped from the holes in the mens' chests. They died with their jaws open in surprise.

Munch tore off the transmitter. It was smoking and smelled like burning plastic. She swung the belt once around her head to pick up speed and then smacked Humberto in the side of the head. The blow put him off balance and then Roger tackled him. Humberto's gun went flying and Munch scrambled after it.

The bodies of Delaguerra and his man jerked back against the side of the Suburban as Christina cut a line of bullet holes across their chests.

When the shooting stopped, the Suburban's alarm went off, sounding long Klaxon bleats. Roger was cuffing Humberto and turned to Munch. "Can you turn that thing off?"

"Sure." She stepped past the bodies on the ground. The driver's door was still open, so she reached in and popped the hood release. Then she quickly located and unplugged the horns.

She returned to where Humberto was sitting on the curb. Roger was emptying the big man's pockets. "By the way, Roger, this is Humberto. Humberto, Roger." He could never say an introduction hadn't taken place.

Now other sirens filled the air, the long-awaited backup was finally arriving.

"You better give me that," Christina said, indicating Humberto's gun still in Munch's hand.

Munch handed it over, grip first.

Ellen poked her head out the front door of Munch's house. "I called the fire department and told them we were going to need some paramedics."

Asia pushed past Ellen and came running across the lawn. Munch had never seen her daughter's face look so pale or her eyes so wide. She wrapped her arms around Asia and turned the little girl's face from the carnage. "It's over now," she said. "We're going to be okay."

St. John arrived with the paramedics and badged his way inside the police cordon that Roger supervised. When he got to Munch and Asia, and realized that none of the blood was theirs, he hugged them in relief. His second reaction was to confront Roger.

"What kind of operation are you running here?" he demanded.

"And you are?" Roger asked.

St. John identified himself.

"This is the narc I told you about," Munch said. "He owes me an explanation and public apology."

Several other DEA agents in blue windbreakers arrived on the scene. They helped Humberto to his feet, treating him with care, and assisted him into the back of Christina's van. She told the other agents that she'd catch a ride with Roger.

"I'm waiting," Munch said.

Christina brushed dirt off her pants, pushed her long hair out of her face, and gave Roger a nod before she began. "Rico got a call from Delaguerra about a week and a half ago. Delaguerra wanted him to help smuggle some guns into the sheriff's lockup in Van Nuys. Several of Delaguerra's soldiers were in custody and looking at going away for a long time. Delaguerra needed help to break them out. Rico was in a spot. If he refused . . . well, let's just say Delaguerra was not a man who took no for an answer."

"Rico went along with the Santiago brothers," Roger said. "The plan was to raid the house where they kept the guns. Take 'em into custody before they hit the street. Rico would get busted along with them to maintain his cover. Then the brothers changed the plan at the last moment, moving up the timetable before we could get the team in place."

"Why didn't he just get out of there?" St. John asked. "Go out for cigarettes or something?"

"The brothers were already suspicious," Christina said. "Rico had run out of excuses. He was hoping some other opportunity would present itself on the way to the lockup. Remember, they had the names and addresses of all his family. We could protect some of them, but never all of them in time. That was Rico's choice."

"Save himself or save his family," Munch said.

"We don't know what exactly happened at the meet," Roger said. "It was too dangerous for him to wear a wire. We heard shots and stormed the house. Rico was already dead and he'd taken out one of the brothers, but the other one was still alive."

"He drew down on our team," Christina said.

Of course he did, St. John thought, but he didn't condemn the agents for shooting the other brother. They had to make their story work.

"We realized we needed to rescript the scenario or Rico would have sacrificed himself for nothing," Roger said.

"So you shot up his body?" Munch asked. "And said he'd been on the wrong side?"

"It was the only way we could protect all of you," Christina said.

"Not to mention your cover," Munch said.

"That's right," she admitted. "He died for me, too."

EPILOGUE:

Seven Months Later . . .

TIME WAS SUPPOSED TO HELP, AND IT HAD, UP TO A POINT. Munch had some good days, but she also had some bad nights. Hour after hour, she would lie alone in her bed, praying for sleep.

There were other lingering effects.

There was a shiny rectangle of scar tissue on the small of Munch's back. The short-circuiting transmitter had charred her skin black. Fourth-degree burns, the doctors said. Munch didn't know there was such a thing. The doctors were surprised to learn that she had never lost consciousness from the pain. They said skin grafts were an option, but she didn't see the point. When she studied her naked back in the mirror, she didn't think it looked so bad. She suspected she was weird for thinking so, but she kind of dug having it.

She had to call Asia if she was going to be even five minutes late or the girl would work herself into a state. Angelica volunteered to baby-sit whenever Munch needed her, and sometimes came over even when Munch wasn't going out.

Munch told Angelica that she would be her stepmother. That Munch could be the person Angelica could always come to when she needed an adult to bounce something off. An adult who wasn't her mother. They didn't tell Sylvia about those conversations. It would only make the woman feel bad, and it wasn't about replacing her as a parent, as much as supplementing. Munch did the same for her nieces and the kids of friends from mostly the old days.

Angelica was keeping her grades up, but according to her teachers, she lacked association skills and tended to keep to herself.

It was an Indian summer that year, the hottest days falling in early autumn. Following a spate of hundred-plus-degree days, Munch woke early on a Saturday morning mid-autumn. The windows were open, letting in the cooler night breeze. She grasped at the wisps of a dream, trying to decipher it, wondering if it was responsible for the sense of urgency she felt. In the dream, her house was sinking in quicksand as she clutched at the windowsills, trying to keep the building up. She had packed her bags to leave. When she tried to pull them through the open window, they alternately wouldn't fit or were too heavy to drag. Someone was trying to tell her something in the most urgent tones, but she was too busy.

Munch checked the clock by her bed. It was four-thirty, yet she was wide awake. At least she had slept a good five hours.

Jasper lifted a sleepy eyelid and regarded her groggily. His jowls hung crooked, one side still flattened by the pillow.

"We have something to do," she said. She went into Asia's room, woke her and told her to dress.

"What is it, Mom?"

"I know there's something we have to do today. I don't remember what." Asia pulled on her clothes without grumbling. Munch loaded them in the car. The dull yellow rays of streetlights broke through the night fog. Munch headed for the freeway, pulled by an impulse she didn't fully understand.

"Where are we going?" Asia asked.

"Looks like to Angelica. She needs to be a part of this."

Angelica was in front of her house when they pulled up. She had put on some much-needed pounds and looked younger. She didn't look surprised to see Munch as she got in the car.

They drove to the beach and parked next to a shuttered concession stand. The sign over the order window was cut and painted to resemble a rainbow.

"This is the place," Munch said.

"What are we supposed to do?" Asia asked.

"Let's walk out to the water. I have some questions." Munch picked up small rocks along the way and handed some of them to the girls. Jasper bounded in front of them, delighted to feel the sand and surf under his paws.

Munch threw one of the rocks at a breaking wave. "I hate feeling this way."

Asia looked at her in surprise.

"I hate it when people I love die." Munch threw another rock. "Why do you let that happen?"

Angelica stepped up next. "You said you'd take care of me forever, and now you're gone." She threw a rock, then two more. "You should have stayed out of my life. Now I miss you."

Asia tossed a rock halfheartedly. "You shouldn't have taken drugs, not when you had a little baby."

Munch was surprised, and honest enough with herself to acknowledge that it hurt her feelings that Asia missed her birth parents.

Angelica stepped up for another turn. "You'll never see me graduate, Daddy, or meet my husband, or—" She stopped talking as her tears overcame her voice.

Asia kicked at the water. She was also crying.

Munch let the girls express themselves. This was not the time for counseling or even comforting. They were here to air their wounds.

"You should have tried harder," Munch said, skimming a flat stone over the surface of a retreating wave. She wasn't talking to Rico now. She knew he had done his best to stay, but it had come to an awful choice, and he showed his love in a way no man from here on after could ever repeat. He'd sacrificed it all for the ones he loved. No, the hurt she was voicing was an old one. A pain she carried like some kind of badge.

The voice from her dream came back to her. She'd been hearing that spokesperson for years, but never quite identified who it was.

She had often woken and wondered at the familiarity of the voice and why she trusted it so completely.

"You're thirty years old," it had said. "It's time to drop this load. Forgive and release."

Munch looked down at Asia as the water swirled around their ankles, and put a hand on her daughter's shoulder. "It's going to be all right." She hugged Angelica to her with her free arm. "We're going to live and love and laugh."

A wave broke offshore and Munch could swear she saw a rainbow in its mist.